ASK ME

M. MALONE

ASK ME © October 2018 M. Malone

Edited by Daisycakes Creative Services

CrushStar Romance

An Imprint of CrushStar Multimedia LLC

Print ISBN: 978-1-938789-45-8

Ebook ISBN: 978-1-938789-44-71

For the real Andre.
You are so much more than I could have ever asked for.
One lifetime with you is not enough.

CONTENTS

ASK ME

THE QUESTION

Andre

I'M THAT GUY.

Yeah, you know the one I'm talking about. The kind women want and other men want to be. Not that I'm complaining. Far from it. This is a charmed life I lead. But there are sacrifices. Anonymity. Privacy. Love.

Things that I didn't know to value highly when I had them.

Don't take that as a complaint by the way. My life is a steady stream of ... whatever the hell I want, actually. Trips around the world, priceless jewels, fast cars, and even faster women.

But lately, I've had more questions than answers. Not to sound too hipster but I just want more. More of what exactly, I'm not sure. Perhaps I'm just trying to understand this circle of life we're all caught in. We wake up, only to work long hours, to eat, sleep and then do it all over again. Friends drift away, family betrays family and then you kick it and leave the results of all your hard work to someone else.

What's the point of all this?

.

.

.

Oh, you're waiting for me to give you an answer? You thought this was why you were here, huh? For me to pull you close, whisper in your ear and tell you all the secrets of success?

Well, I can't do that. Not that I don't want to. I'd show you where the keys to the castle were hidden if I knew. But I don't. Haven't you figured that out yet? That's why we're *both* here.

Because I don't fucking know.

Andre

AESTHETICS ARE EVERYTHING. YES, WE'VE ALL HEARD the usual drivel. What is it that people always say?

Beauty is in the eye of the beholder.

Beauty is only skin deep.

Well, ladies and gentlemen, I hate to be the bearer of bad news but those people are liars. After all, I've never seen anyone at a beauty pageant put the crown on a sweet personality.

No, it's what's on the outside that counts in this cutthroat world and we've turned the pursuit of beauty into a cross-cultural obsession. Humanity has always appreciated beauty, this is true, but never before have we made it so socially acceptable to crave it. In the past it was considered a sin to covet attractiveness but now people live stream going to the plastic surgeon's office to get a nose job. It's trendy to chase beauty.

And I would know all about it. I'm famous for creating the trends the world loves to chase.

My eyes move around the room without really taking any of it in. All I get is an impression of opulence: high ceilings, glittering chandeliers and soft light. The scene could easily come from a movie. The ballroom in the hotel is the height of elegance with marble floors and tall doors leading out to balconies that overlook the gardens. Waiters roam the crowd offering all manner of culinary delights and an endless stream of champagne. I'm surrounded by beauty.

Too bad I couldn't give less than a damn about any of it.

A man steps into my path and holds out his hand to shake. "Mr. Lavin. Pleasure to see you here. I'm Timothy Armand."

Not given much of a choice, I accept the handshake with resignation. It was foolish to think that I'd get a few moments alone to gather my thoughts before the wolves descended. The man is young with light brown hair slicked back with far too much pomade and is wearing a black suit that is definitely off the rack. The sleeves are slightly too short and the inseam is so high I'm surprised he's not a soprano by now.

"Sir, your last collection was transcendent. I'm a designer, too. Right now I work for Posture, an up-and-coming fashion blog. Would you be willing—"

I paste on a smile. "All interview requests need to go through my assistant. Call the office and we'll get you scheduled." After a quick pat on the back, I leave him still stammering after me.

Everyone at the 22nd Annual International Fashion World Gala is wearing one-of-a-kind creations designed to showcase their skill and creativity. I recognize most of the other attendees as either my colleagues, competitors or models who work frequently in the industry. Our community is a small but competitive one and it's important to know your environment. If this event had been for any other organization, I would have skipped it and spent the night romancing a bottle of scotch.

Tonight, I'm wearing a traditional tuxedo; however, instead of silk or satin on the lapels, I used feathers. Each one is hand stitched to create the effect of wings. The theme for tonight's gala is "Animal Instincts" and some of my peers have taken it quite seriously. A woman glides by wearing a bodycon dress that is so tight its panther design looks like her skin color. I turn slightly to watch her progress and then have to hold in a laugh when I see the ribbon around her waist has been braided in the back to mimic a panther's tail.

Interesting.

This is the part that keeps me coming back. I live for the ingenuity and creativity fashion design is known for. It's what kept me going when no one knew who I was or cared. I was fortunate to come from a wealthy family but with wealth often comes certain expectations. Fashion is not the career my parents would have chosen and in the beginning they didn't even pretend to hide their disappointment. They came around later but the early days were rough.

This is not an easy business to enter without a support system.

I turn and catch sight of the young man I met earlier. Timothy. He's standing alone and looking around the room with trepidation. He doesn't appear to know anyone here. My mind flashes back to the first time I attended this gala. No one made the effort to make me feel welcome either.

Damn it.

I grab another flute of champagne from a passing waiter. Timothy's eyes spark as I approach.

"Don't get discouraged if no one will talk to you. They didn't talk to me either when I first arrived on the scene ten years ago. Most of the people I met were twats, actually."

His mouth falls open slightly before he chokes out a surprised laugh. "Good to know. I was wondering if I had bad breath or something."

At least he's got a sense of humor. He's leagues ahead of

where I was when I started. I spent far too many years caring about what the people in this room thought of me.

"When you call my office, tell them to put you on the new designers list. You'll get scheduled faster that way."

Every few months, I make it a point to reach out to newer designers. They can ask questions or simply get my opinion on something they're working on. Mentorship is something I feel strongly about and it benefits me, too. Seeing what the next generation in fashion is doing keeps me fresh and challenges me not to get complacent.

"Thank you, sir." He pumps my hand enthusiastically and despite my general dislike of interviews, I make a mental note to save something special to show him when we meet again.

I remember all too well what it's like to be just starting out and hungry for someone, anyone, to give you a chance.

Walking faster now, I pause briefly to compliment an old friend on the dress his model is wearing. The double doors leading to the balcony loom ahead and I let out a sigh of relief as I reach for the handle.

"Andre. Where are you going, *mio figlio*?"

And ... denied.

"Evening, Mamma." My hand drops from the handle of the doors as I turn around.

My mother narrows her eyes slightly as she looks between me and the doors. "You weren't leaving already, were you?

7

I've told you, networking is so important. Now more than ever."

"Of course. I was only going to get some air. It can get quite stifling at these events."

She waves that away with an impatient hand. "No time for that now. There's someone I want you to meet."

It's an effort to hold in a long-suffering sigh but I follow behind dutifully as she leads me toward the center of the room. Fashion designer wasn't exactly Sofia Lavin's first choice of career for her eldest son but she has invested large amounts of the money she inherited from her parents into my business. Making nice with her friends is the least I can do. I'll just say hello and then make my escape.

"Here he is!" My mother pauses next to a group of people and I struggle to arrange my face into something resembling interest.

"Andre, this is Mr. Gabriel Knight and his wife, Hannah." My mother turns to a young, blond woman standing right behind them. "And this is their lovely daughter, Elisabetta."

The young woman steps forward and when she sees me the look of boredom on her face vanishes instantly. She tucks a stray curl behind her ear nervously. "Oh hello! It's so nice to meet you. Your mother has told us so much about you. I feel like we're old friends already!"

My mother moves so that Elisabetta can step closer. When our eyes meet, my mother shrugs innocently.

Escape isn't going to come easily.

By the time I get away, it's an hour later and I'm wishing the feathers around my neck could actually fly me away. I finally gave up all semblance of civility and just walked away from Elisabetta mid-sentence. I'm not the most patient man even on a good day and right now I need some air. Her fake laugh and cloying perfume gave me a headache.

When I finally push my way through the crowd to reach the balcony doors, the humid air slaps me in the face. I'm probably going to regret my choice of attire tonight—tuxedos and humidity don't mix—but I'm too happy to escape the horde inside to care. Hell, I'd rather sweat out here alone than be comfortable in the air conditioning in the midst of vultures.

But as I step closer to the railing, I become aware that I'm not alone. My mood plummets until I recognize the man hiding in the shadows. His dark hair, the exact same shade as mine, is tousled and there's an unlit cigarette clamped between his lips.

"You're hiding out too, I see."

My younger brother, Philippe, straightens slightly and flashes a tight smile. "Mamma is driving me crazy. I had to make up an excuse to get away." He takes the cigarette from between his teeth. "I don't even smoke."

We both chuckle at that. I'm not surprised he's willing to feign nicotine addiction. It's actually rather brilliant. Maybe I should come up with a convenient excuse for why I need to step outside often. That could turn out to be quite useful considering my mother's current mission to shove every woman she knows of childbearing age in my direction. I hadn't realized Philippe was getting the same treatment.

"At least you found somewhere to hide. I got caught and just spent the last hour talking to a woman who has no further ambition in life than wearing more expensive shoes than her friends."

Suddenly it all comes down on me and I am tired. I feel like a piece of fabric that has been stretched until it's frayed and thin. And I'm starting to not even recognize myself.

"Do you ever get tired of this?" I gesture around us. "Tired of the fake people, the gossip, the drama?"

He shrugs. "Of course. But what can you do? This is part of our world and always has been. Remember when Papa was alive and he would throw those parties?"

Now that brings a genuine smile to my face. My parents used to entertain frequently and, of course, Philippe and I were required to attend the events. The world we were born into is obsessed with social standing and appearances. My father never seemed to enjoy those parties the way my mother did. For him, it was a labor of love for the woman he adored.

"How I hated those parties. And now … "

"Now you would give anything to attend just to see him again." Philippe nods in understanding. "Believe me, I know. He would be proud of you, you know?"

The statement hits me square in the chest. There's a part of me that wonders if he would be. Not about me. I know that he loved me. But sometimes I get a sick feeling when I imagine what he'd think of my newfound fame and all the accolades I've racked up.

Nicholas Lavin was not a flashy man or even one who basked in the limelight. He was a quiet man who fell in love with a woman from a different social class. He worked night and day to make his financial services company the best so he could prove himself worthy of her. Nothing can ever touch the memories I have of him. No matter how busy he was, he always made time for his family. And he loved my mother with all his heart until the day he died.

"This isn't exactly what he wanted for us. I think he tried to steer us on the path of integrity instead of chasing money and status. If high society hadn't been so important to Mamma, I think he would have gladly given it all up to go live quietly in the country somewhere."

Philippe tilts his head slightly as he looks at me. After a moment, it makes me uncomfortable. I love my brother, partially because he's one of the few people in the world that truly knows me. Which can be simultaneously heartwarming and annoying. Especially moments like this when my emotions are churning and I'm not even sure what I'm feeling.

"You've been unhappy for quite some time. I'd hoped you'd figure out the why and move on but I don't see that happening." He leans against the railing and looks out at the view of the city. "You can talk to me. You know that, right?"

"I do know that. If I knew what to say, I would. I'm just ... tired, I suppose."

He raises an eyebrow at that. "This is coming from the man who rarely sleeps? What's really going on with you? Look at all that you've achieved. All that you've done. What more could you want?"

His voice is soft which blunts the harsh tone of the questions. It makes it easier for me to truly think about the answers. What do I want? Everything I've ever wanted is now within reach. Is that not the definition of happiness? I think of the penthouse apartment that is being readied for me even as we speak. Just a few years ago I would have been excited about it. But now it's just one more piece of real estate that I've acquired.

Just another empty home to fill.

"It all seems so pointless. I've done so much but at the end of the day I'm still alone with no one to share it with. The people I spend the most time with are on my payroll. Every smile, every conversation, is part of their workday. All I ever wanted was success but now that it's here, it brings its own problems."

He sighs. "I know that day on the red carpet affected you."

My hands clench on the balcony rail. "Not talking about that."

The idea that a young fan almost lost her life because of her obsession with me isn't something I'm ready to deal with.

Security moved quickly to contain the situation and my team was able to keep the worst details of the incident out of the news. However, there are still a few who know what happened. Kate has been monitoring the young girl's care and we anonymously donated money to help her. Every once in a while someone tries to talk about it with me but I'm just not ready to go there yet.

Philippe shakes his head. "I hear you, brother. But this is the life we lead. The money will always attract people who want things. But what's the alternative? I'm sure poor men have it much harder. Try meeting a woman as a regular guy. Take off the perfectly tailored suit and the Rolex."

Suddenly he laughs so hard that he bends at the waist trying to catch his breath. "*Dio*, I can't even imagine it. You wouldn't last a day if you had to wear an off-the-rack suit."

I scowl but it's hard to maintain my anger while he's chuckling. "So I'm a snob, is that what you're saying?"

He claps me on the shoulder. "No. You know I don't think that. But you have very exacting standards. I wonder what would happen if you allowed yourself to have even a little bit of fun sometimes. You might even enjoy yourself for once. Try it. I dare you."

His eyes suddenly go to something over my shoulder. "I have to go. If I see Mamma, I'll try to distract her for you. Give you a few more minutes of peace."

The balcony doors shut behind him and finally, I'm alone.

Not that I would ever admit it to him, but his words pierced me to my core. He didn't mean anything by it but seeing myself through his eyes was a bit shocking.

Am I really that bad?

Perhaps I have become jaded over the years, so used to all the finer things in life, but I don't think I've lost touch with reality. We've always had money so one could argue we've never exactly been regular people but there was a time I was considered the life of the party, entertaining and enjoying friendships with people from all walks of life. But as my career grew, my leisure time dwindled and then became nonexistent.

And so did my fun.

Fun is the one thing that I can definitely say is missing in my life. All work and no play would make anyone unhappy.

Add in the stress of maintaining a public image, especially one as high profile as mine, and it's no wonder I'm feeling out of sorts. I need to go back to the way things used to be, when I was just starting out and no one knew my name. My friends were there because they liked me and not because I could get them entree into exclusive parties or get them followers on Instagram. I was happy then.

Suddenly, the idea that seemed so ridiculous when Philippe said it is all I can think about. Going out into the world and having a little fun outside of the exclusive bubble I live in.

That's a dare I'm willing to take.

2

Andre

THE NEXT FEW WEEKS ARE BRUTAL AND I DON'T HAVE time to do anything other than make sure the empire I've built doesn't fall. But off and on, Philippe's idea plants itself in my mind and spreads its roots through my imagination.

The idea is too tantalizing to ignore. And I've always been a sucker for a dare. I send a message to my assistant to have a few things waiting for me at my hotel and then promptly forget about it.

Until there's a knock on the door on a random Friday afternoon.

My mind runs blank for a moment as I try to remember

which luxury hotel I'm staying in this week. It's not fashion week so that narrows things down a bit. I open the door to Reginald, the concierge at this hotel. My memory is still fuzzy until my eyes fall to the discreet Fitz-Harrington logo on the plastic bag in Reginald's hand.

Ah, that clears it up. I'm in the States again. I only stay at the Fitz when I'm in Washington, D.C.

"Your requests, sir. I hope you'll find them satisfactory."

"You were able to find everything?"

He looks stricken. "Of course, Mr. Lavin. Well, I didn't go personally but one of the maids lives in Virginia and was willing to visit ... " He lowers his voice. " ... *Wal-Mart* to pick these up for you on the way in to work this morning."

Reginald presents me with the bag reluctantly, as if the items I've asked for are so unsavory that he can't bear to sully his hands.

The thought makes me smile. You'd think I asked him to procure hookers or drugs by the look on his face. Instead the bag should contain a pair of jeans, a plain cotton T-shirt and a pair of Nike athletic shoes in size eleven.

"Thank you, Reginald."

As I take the bag, I discreetly slip him some money. He doesn't blink so that must mean I got it right and gave him dollars this time instead of euros. Traveling so much, it's easy to get confused occasionally about which cash to use when or what language to speak where. Although I have to give Reginald credit. When I spoke to him in Italian upon arrival, he responded as if he understood so he must have a working knowledge of several languages.

I do appreciate excellent service.

Trying not to appear too eager, I close the door gently and carry the bag to the bed. The first thing I pull out is the T-shirt. It's actually a bundle containing three separate colors: white, red and black. I decide on the white one. My brow furrows at the thought of wearing this rough material next to my skin but I quickly forget about that when my hands land on the denim. It's stiff and much thinner than I expected. But hell, it's not like I'll be wearing them for that long.

It only takes me a few minutes to change clothes. The shoes fit perfectly and are very comfortable. The finishing touch is a baseball cap given to me by the head of my advertising agency. As the creator and namesake of my own fashion line, people give me clothing all the time. Designers who want to work for me, rivals who want to crush me, you name it. But it's not that often I get a gift just because. At the time, I found it amusing since sports have never been my thing but I'm glad I held on to it.

It completes the perfect disguise.

The presidential suites have their own elevator so I make it downstairs quickly. This will be the real test. Whether I can walk out without anyone calling my bluff. My heart pounds as I cross the marble lobby, the new sneakers sticking slightly. But no one says anything and no one stops me. A few seconds later I'm standing outside, blinking into the sunshine. Part of me wants to cheer but my feet keep moving, traversing the concrete walk that takes me away from the hotel and into the stream of people outside walking to their destinations.

I laugh aloud. Now that I've "escaped" I realize that I don't know where to go. My plan didn't extend much further than my disguise. The bright yellow of a taxicab catches my eye and I raise my hand to hail it. I can always go get some coffee and then figure out where to go next from there. I haven't found a coffee shop in America yet that can produce a decent espresso but there's a small cafe near my advertising agency that does a fine cappuccino.

It's an experience riding through the streets of DC and my senses are attuned to take it all in. Over the past few years, all I've done is work with single-minded focus on expanding my fashion brand and achieving my dreams. Now I have everything I ever wanted but none of it seems to mean a damn.

Ennui is what the French call it. Boredom. A dissatisfaction with life in general. Something that makes no sense when you've finally gotten everything you want.

The taxi pulls over in front of the coffee shop and I hand over several bills. Once I hop out, someone is climbing into the cab before I even clear the door. The young woman doesn't say "excuse me" or even look at me. A smile tugs at the edges of my lips. It's not often I feel invisible.

Normal, I remind myself. *This is what it's like to be normal.*

Lately, there's been something angry inside of me, a dissatisfaction that has only spread. It's like I'm looking for something but I don't know what it is or how to find it. But I've had a growing feeling lately that what I've been looking for is connection. I'm surrounded by people constantly who want something from me or want to *be* me. But rarely anyone who sees beneath the surface.

As I stand there on the curb, watching people flow around me, it hits me that I could just walk away from it all. Right now. I tilt my face up and enjoy the sensation of the sun on my face. It's strange to just stand here, enjoying the moment, having nowhere to be, no appointments to keep, no investors to impress. When was the last time I did something just for the fun of it or for the delight of trying something new? How long has it been since I was free to be just Andre, instead of Andre Lavin, fashion mogul and internet sensation?

How long since I really lived?

Too long, I decide. Maybe this is crazy. When my brother dared me to try picking up a woman like a normal guy, I thought it would just be a little bit of fun. But the more I think about it, the more the thought resonates. What if I wasn't Andre Lavin, reigning emperor of fashion?

What if I was just ... me?

My existential crisis in the middle of the sidewalk is interrupted when a mother pushing a huge stroller rolls over my foot. She offers an apology. Then she asks for my number. I accept the first and refuse the second before limping into the coffee shop. Hopefully, a shot of sugar straight to my veins will help. That's essentially what the drinks that Americans call "coffee" are anyway, milk and sugar boiled together with a small bit of actual coffee thrown in for good measure.

With gritted teeth I order a latte. When in Rome, as they say.

By the time I have my coffee in hand, the pain in my foot has subsided enough and I decide to take a walk. My advertising agency is right across the street, but I definitely can't go there looking like this. But I can walk around and enjoy the weather and the opportunity to do nothing. Before I left, I turned my cell phone off (something I never do), and I can only imagine how many emails and calls are being ignored right now. The thought gives me a little bit of forbidden satisfaction.

On the way out of the coffee shop, I sip the latte and try

not to wince at the overly sweet taste. Suddenly, something slams into my stomach and I have to juggle to keep my hot coffee from flying out of my hands.

"Ouch!"

A mass of brown hair slaps me in the face before it settles around a heart-shaped face dominated by a pair of big, amber eyes. Those eyes blink at me several times before it registers that she's leaning unsteadily against me.

"In a hurry?"

At the sound of my voice, her eyes latch on to mine before she takes a slight step back. Her cheeks flush slightly before her eyes scroll leisurely up and down my body. Somehow her gaze is as provocative as a physical touch would have been. By the time she gets back to my face, my heart is tripping over itself and my mouth is dry as dust. What the hell?

"Yes, I am. I'm very busy and ... have lots of important things I need to do this morning."

Her insistence is even more adorable because she flushes bright red as she says it. She's obviously not a very good liar. Which is refreshing.

"Is that right?" I raise my eyebrows playfully, enjoying the chance to tease her a little. Hey, she just stared at my dick. I don't think a little teasing is out of bounds.

"Yes, really." She huffs a little, tugging on the bottom of her skirt as if making sure it hasn't ridden up. Petite but curvy, she looks like she's about to rip through the buttons on her blouse if she breathes too deeply. I wonder if she's outgrown her clothes or borrowed them from someone else. Either way, they don't do her justice.

"Oh no," she gasps, her eyes fixed on the front of my shirt. "Did I do that?"

I glance down to see the remains of my caffè latte all over my T-shirt. Normally a brown stain like this would be the death knell for a piece of fabric but it hits me suddenly the other benefit of wearing these ugly clothes. If the cleaners can't get the stain out, I'll just throw it away and buy another T-shirt. The thought makes me smile.

Her brow crinkles in confusion before she rummages in the huge bag hanging off her arm and produces two napkins. "I am so sorry. But you don't seem too upset about it."

"I'm not. The coffee was shit anyway. I'm still not sure how Americans drink that stuff. Give me a good strong espresso any day instead of that sugar water."

Her answering smile is so bright that I have the urge to shade my eyes. Looking at her is like staring into the sun. I want to but it's just too much for my eyes to take in. The thought is perplexing. She's beautiful, yes, but I see beautiful women all the time. Occupational hazard.

But those women aren't talking with you for no reason.

The women in my world always want something, to be cast in one of my runway shows or to be on my arm at a movie premiere. This one doesn't care about any of that. She's smiling for no reason at all.

She turns to leave but there's a trash can right behind her. I put a hand on her shoulder to keep her from bumping into it and she glares at me. I snatch my hand back.

"Just trying to keep you from running into something else."

Her eyes narrow but then she glances behind her. "Oh. Thank you."

She waves and then keeps walking. I turn to watch her go, suppressing a low growl when I see her curvy ass twitching in that tight little skirt.

"*Madre di Dio.*"

3

Casey

THE FATE OF MY FUTURE LIES IN THE HANDS OF THE MAN sitting in front of me. I silently send up a little prayer to the patron saint of screwups.

James Lawson is the head of a fancy marketing agency and my only chance at getting a job. All of the other companies I contacted didn't bother to call me back. I suppose my resume wasn't that impressive. Not surprising with its grand total of half a degree and two jobs including waitressing and three weeks as an office assistant at Bob's Car Wash.

It's hard not to stare so I focus my eyes on his tie instead.

It's a deep maroon color and there's a silver thread running through it that makes it look expensive.

Everyone I've met since moving to the "big city" looks expensive.

"So, tell me about yourself, Cassandra." James smiles kindly, folding his hands on top of his desk.

"Of course. Well, everyone calls me Casey. I just moved here from a little town called Gracewell, Virginia. I'm excited to finish my marketing degree and gain some valuable experience in the industry at the same time."

He listens attentively to my well-rehearsed spiel and I can only hope he doesn't notice that my voice shakes slightly. When I made the impromptu decision to move to Washington, D.C., I was high on adrenalin and humiliation. I have a knack for catastrophe and the past two years have been particularly brutal. Halfway through my college career, I was doing well, keeping my grades up and happy with my boyfriend. Until I discovered that the man I thought I was going to marry was already married to someone else.

All the stress affected my grades until I had to withdraw from school. My mom barely scraped together the money to send me in the first place; she definitely couldn't afford to pay for classes that I wasn't going to pass. At the time, getting a job seemed like the best plan. Until my new boss heard the rumors about why I left school and figured I was fair game. When I rejected him, he told everyone I came on to *him*.

I guess when you have a reputation as a home-wrecker, the truth no longer matters. People in Gracewell believe I had an affair with my boss and nothing, certainly not the truth, was going to convince them otherwise.

My shoulders slump slightly. Honestly, being this much of a fuck-up is kind of exhausting. Worse, was knowing that my mom had to hear those rumors. It wasn't easy for her to return to her hometown, pregnant and unmarried, and I think her worst nightmare is watching me go down the same path.

But that's why I'm here. After two years of working at the diner, I enrolled in online classes and made a decision. I knew if I didn't get out of Gracewell now, I'd end up settling down with one of the guys I went to high school with and finishing my degree would be just one more dream I never got to fulfill. I'm determined not to allow that to happen.

I'm twenty-three years old. It's now or never.

"Well, I can see that you have some experience as an assistant and that you worked as a waitress through high school and for the past two years. So you have customer service experience. Excellent."

I blink in surprise. It almost sounds like he's helping me, spinning my sparse work experience to make it sound more impressive.

"Yes, I dealt with all types of people working at the diner. Most of them were regulars but we have a lot of truckers who would stop through as well. They had some of the best stories."

James nods along enthusiastically. "Fantastic. That's exactly what we need here at Mirage. A friendly face that can engage all of our different clients. We'd love for you to start right away, if that works for you?"

I nod in disbelief and before I can process what's going on, he's on his feet. Not sure exactly what's happening, I stand awkwardly and grab my bag before following. The next ten minutes are a whirlwind of handshakes and smiles as James introduces me to Hannah from HR, and a bunch of other people whose names escape me.

"And now I'll leave you with Anya who is going to handle your training."

For a moment, I just stand there with my mouth hanging open, trying to figure out what happened between sitting down for the interview and now.

"Are you okay?" Anya asks after I've been standing there blinking for a few moments.

"Yes. Just not sure if this is real. I didn't think I'd actually get the job. I don't have fancy experience, not the type I thought I'd need to work here."

Anya's smile softens. "I'll tell you a little secret. We've had horrible luck with all the receptionists we hired through the temp agency. And all of those people had the 'fancy' experience. I think James is just looking for someone who is not crazy and can work the phone system at this point."

That makes me laugh. "I think the jury is still out on the not crazy part but the phone system—that I can handle."

Anya crosses her arms. "I have a feeling you're going to fit in really well here. Come on, I'll introduce you around."

I follow her in a daze, still not sure if this is really happening. Ever since I arrived in the city three days ago, it's been one disappointment after the other. First, the perfectly normal hotel I booked online turned out to be a crappy motel in what is apparently one of the worst neighborhoods in the city. I figured out just what kind of place it was on day one when I tried to leave my room and found a girl giving some guy a blow job. Just right there in the parking lot.

If it wasn't so gross, I could almost be impressed. That lady clearly had skin of steel if she could handle kneeling on asphalt.

Then I got my next shock on day two when I attempted to visit the apartment listings I found online. It turns out that having the first and last month of rent isn't good enough. They wanted recent pay stubs to prove that I had a job. Which leads me to today. This interview was super important because I needed a job to get out of the hellhole motel so I'd stayed up all night researching the Mirage agency and reviewing all my notes from my marketing classes. That explains why I overslept slightly and almost ran over that cute guy on the way here.

My face flushes again at the memory. He really had been cute which made the whole thing even more mortifying. Luckily he hadn't seemed all that concerned about dropping his coffee or the huge brown stain it left all over his T-shirt. I would have offered to pay for the dry cleaning but considering how expensive everything is in the city, I probably couldn't afford it.

You should have offered to pay. Then you would have had an excuse to get his number. Or give him yours.

No. I mentally shut that down. That's the kind of thinking that always lands me in hot water. I'm here to get away from guy drama not create more.

I focus as Anya leads me down another hallway and then stops to poke her head into an office. "Mya, do you have a second?"

A gorgeous woman with glowing bronze skin and a long black braid looks up from her computer screen.

"This is Casey. Casey, this is Mya, one of the team leads. She handles quite a few of our luxury brands."

Mya lets out a little squeal. "Please save my life right now and tell me James finally hired someone?"

Anya looks over at me. "See? I told you. Everyone is really happy you're here. The last temp we had got everyone's messages wrong and used to eat tuna fish sandwiches every day."

"Well, I'm glad to be here. Nothing else has gone right since I moved so it's nice to finally feel welcome somewhere."

Mya closes her laptop and stands. "Oh are you new to the city?"

"Brand new. I got here three days ago and quickly learned that the pictures online can be very deceiving. My hotel looks more like a hostel from one of those horror movies. And I'm pretty sure some guy got murdered in the parking lot last night."

Anya winces. "Oh yikes. I can ask my landlord if there are any openings in my building."

Mya peers at me. "Do you smoke?"

I shake my head. "No. My mom's a nurse. She would kill me if she ever caught even a whiff of cigarette smoke on me."

"Your mom is a nurse? This must be fate. My old roommate just posted an ad looking for someone to take my room. She's a nurse, too. Let me see if she found someone yet." She's already pulled her phone out of her pocket.

A few seconds later the phone rings, blaring out a rap song. Mya curses softly before answering, silencing the raunchy lyrics. "Damn it, Ariana. You can't keep changing my ringtone. I am at work!"

"Put me on speaker." The voice on the other end is so loud that we can hear her anyway. Mya pulls the phone away from her ear slightly. "Fine, hold on." She glances over at me. "Sorry about this. She's a little pushy."

"I can hear you!" The voice shouts.

Mya pushes another button and then angles the phone toward me. "Ok, Ari. You're on speaker now. This is Casey. Be nice to her. She's the first normal receptionist we've had in ages."

The voice chuckles. "Normal is boring. Hey chick, do you have a lot of bill collectors after you? Car that got repossessed? Credit card bills?"

I look over at Mya uncertainly who just shrugs.

"No. I don't own a car and I'm pretty frugal. I don't actually own much. Just a suitcase filled with old books and some clothes that don't fit that well anymore."

She harrumphs at that. "Weird habits? Pick your teeth? Clip your toenails at the table? Sleepwalking?"

"No, no, and I'm not sure. I mean, if I'm asleep, would I really know?"

The line is quiet.

"Ok, one final question. This is *really* important." She pauses. "Who would you bang: Chris Hemsworth, Chris Evans, Chris Pratt or Chris Pine?"

"Um, all of the above?"

A cackle of laughter comes over the line. "Hot damn. You're the first person to pass the Chris test. Everyone always picks one as if they'd *really* turn down any of the others.

Would *you* trust a chick who wouldn't bang one of those guys?"

"Oh good grief," Mya interrupts. "I'll call you later, Ari." She hangs up and puts her phone back in her pocket. "I am so sorry about that. I thought she was going to ask you real questions about paying the rent and stuff."

I wave away her concerns. "No problem, I'm grateful to have a chance to escape the Homicide Hotel."

She rolls her eyes. "You might not be so grateful after living with Ariana for awhile. The chick is insane. Come on. I'll take you to meet the rest of the marketing team."

I follow behind her, trying not to show just how nervous and excited I am right now.

Finally, something is going right.

The rest of the afternoon goes quickly. There's a lot to be done since James apparently wants me to start immediately. After filling out all the employment forms, authorizing a background check and signing what feels like a metric ton of paperwork, Anya shows me where I'll be sitting and how to log in to the company network.

"Are you guys finished for the day?" Mya leans over the front desk where Anya is showing me the list of all the company extensions. Whenever someone calls in, I'm responsible for transferring them to the right party. Some of the names are highlighted. Those are the people who get the most calls, Anya explained.

"Just about done," Anya responds with a warm smile for me. "I'm so damn excited not to have to man this desk alone anymore I could sing."

"Take your time. Ariana said that we could come by anytime after six."

"Wait, it's after six?" Anya hops up, pushing a hand through her hair. "I didn't realize we'd been at it for so long. I think we're good here. Casey, I'll see you tomorrow." With a wave, she rushes off down the hallway to the back offices.

I let out a sigh of relief.

"Don't let her overwhelm you," Mya whispers conspiratorially. "Anya has enough energy for ten people."

"Good to know. And thank you again for letting me know about the apartment. It'll be a relief not to have to live with a complete stranger."

"I agree. I was super lucky when I found Ari by chance but I've had plenty of awful roommates over the years. Finding one who isn't going to steal your stuff or murder you in your sleep is almost as hard as finding a boyfriend."

She waits patiently while I log out of my computer and gather my handbag from the drawer I placed it in earlier.

We chat easily about all the people I met on my first day as we walk outside into the early evening sunshine and Mya hails us a cab. Envious of how easily she does it, I have to push down a little flash of nervousness. Mya is one of those women who make it all seem so easy. Beautiful, successful and self-assured, she doesn't seem like the type who'd ever get herself into the kinds of situations I'm known for. Someone like her would never let herself be taken advantage of and she certainly wouldn't run away at the first sign of trouble.

Stop it. You did what you thought was best. Now it's time to move on and build a life that you can be proud of.

Oblivious to my internal struggles, Mya points out buildings of interest as we pass and jokes around with the cab driver when he almost sideswipes another car. When the car finally pulls over, she gestures around us.

"This neighborhood is called Adams Morgan. It's a great location if you're into nightlife. Lots of restaurants and bars within walking distance."

The building has an elevator but Mya heads straight for the stairs. When we reach the third floor I'm ashamed that I'm panting a little. No wonder the buttons on my shirt are too tight! I put a hand to my head, patting at the moisture there.

Mya notices me lagging behind and pauses to let me catch up. "Are you okay?"

"Yeah, sorry. I just didn't want to meet my potential new roommate looking like a sweaty, out-of-shape mess. I want to make a good first impression."

Mya snorts. "You don't need to worry about that."

I pause. "What does that mean?"

"You'll see. Just ... don't judge too harshly on the first meeting. Ari is a little kooky but she has a heart of gold and means well. Mostly."

Wait. *Mostly?*

A door swings open and a woman darts into the hall wearing a wet suit and carrying a snorkel. Her blond hair is bundled up in a sloppy bun that somehow still makes her look like a supermodel. When she sees us in the hall, she blinks. Then blinks again.

"Oh. It's just you."

I glance over at Mya uncertainly. She sighs. "Ari, this is Casey Michaels. Casey, this is Ariana Silva. And why do you seem surprised to see us? You told me to come by after six, you nutball."

My eyes are ping-ponging between them, sure the woman in the wet suit will take offense to that. But she just smiles prettily before putting her snorkel on.

"You always say you get off at six and then you come at like nine. I just figured you had your numbers upside down or something. Or that you and Triple H were spending the extra hours putting the 6 and the 9 together for some good 'ole fashioned simultaneous loving. I can't be mad at that."

I'm trying to hold my laugh in since Mya doesn't look amused but it's hard. "Triple H?" I ask.

Ari grins. "It stands for Happy Hour Hottie. Because Mya and her hubby started their love affair at the office happy hour when she caught him in the bathroom where some chick had her hand on his–"

"Okay, let's just move this inside. I'm sure the neighbors don't want to hear this." Mya looks appalled but Ariana just rolls her eyes.

"I bet they do," she responds. "Mrs. Abernathy down the hall is a little freak. She had two guys coming out of her apartment last night so she can't judge."

"They were probably repairmen, Ari." Mya shakes her head but she's laughing too. She glances over at me. "Mrs. Abernathy is eighty years old at least."

"So what? Older ladies need lovin' too. And repairmen?" Ari gives her a knowing look. "Isn't that how every porno starts? Ding dong! Hello, ma'am. I'm here to lay the pipe." She pumps her hips in a lewd dance.

I'm pretty sure my mouth is dragging on the ground by now but I follow them into the apartment.

"What about you? You have a boyfriend?" Ari asks. It takes me a moment to realize she's talking to me. Despite trying to play it cool, I'm sure the expression on my face says it all.

"Uh, no. I'm on sort of a man-hiatus right now. I think I have bad luck where relationships are concerned."

Ari nods sagely. "I hear that. Most dudes aren't really

worth the effort anyway. Besides, you know how they say men won't buy the cow if they get the milk for free? Well, I say why buy the pig when all you want is a little sausage?"

Mya turns to me. "I apologize for my former roommate. I tried to warn you but I think I forgot how off the rails she could be. I hope we haven't scared you off."

Ari doesn't look repentant in the least as she grins at us before putting her mouthpiece back in and breathing like Darth Vader. She kind of reminds me of my best friend from high school. Outrageous and fun but if you just went with the flow, she was the most loyal friend ever.

"You definitely haven't scared me off. Honestly, I haven't had this much fun in a long time."

"See? She's fine." Ari looks triumphant. "Come on, I'll show you around."

The main living area is painted a soft cream color and all the furniture looks cozy and lived in. A little dog with black and white fur snoozes on a chair in the corner. Ari points out the kitchen and then shows me the second bedroom. Everything is bright and clean and the room even comes furnished. Mya left a lot of her furniture when she got married since she didn't need it, Ari explains.

Despite how wild our introduction was, Ariana seems like she'll be an ideal roommate. She works at the hospital and only occasionally has night shift so I doubt she'll keep me awake by coming in late or ultra early. The place looks clean but not so clean that I worry she'll kick me out if I forget to wash a glass after I use it. It seems normal. Completely normal.

And for the first time since I left home, I think that things are going to be okay.

"So, what do you think?" Mya asks. "Not to put you on the spot or anything. I'm sure you had other apartments you wanted to look at."

"I'll take it. But there's just one thing." I look over at Ariana. "Do you know anyplace close by where I could apply for a waitressing position? I don't have a car so I need something that I can walk to if possible."

Ari nods. "Yeah. I know a place that just put a sign up last week looking for help."

"Great. Also, I'm almost afraid to ask but if we're going to be roommates, we might as well get it all out there. Were you expecting someone? I know you said most men aren't worth the effort but ... " I gesture to her outfit. "If this is a weird sex game you play with your temporary *sausage*, I can handle that. Just put a snorkel on the door if you don't want me to come in."

Ariana takes the snorkel off. "Oh, I like her. This is going to work out just fine."

4

Andre

THE SKETCHES ON MY DESK BLUR BEFORE MY EYES. Physically I'm still sitting in my office, behind the same desk I bought five years ago after our first favorable review. But I'm not seeing the designs for our next fashion show; instead, just more work that will lead to more sleepless nights.

My little adventure yesterday put me behind and I've been playing catchup all morning. I run my hands through my hair. The clock on the wall across from me taunts me with the early hour. It feels like I've been behind this desk for an entire workday already and it's not even close to lunchtime.

The door opens, bringing in a rush of sound. Philippe

walks in carrying a to-go cup of coffee and his tablet. He pauses when he sees the look on my face.

"Are they that bad?" He glances down at my desk and I realize after a moment that he means the sketches.

"No. Of course not. Our design team is the best."

"Then why do you look so ... " He pauses. "I can't even describe the look on your face."

"It's nothing. I'm just tired."

He takes a seat in the chair across from me and rests his ankle casually on his knee. That's my brother, always calm, cool and without a care in the world. It's something I envy about him, his ability to let everything go and just enjoy the moment. He doesn't stress over the little things the way I do.

As if he can read my thoughts, he points at me. "You're stressed. All you do is work lately and you never want to go out. Look at us, Andre. We're young. We're hot. We're rich. There should be no worries."

"That easy, huh? Someone has to work hard to keep this whole ship running." I smile so he knows I'm teasing.

Despite his dilettante lifestyle, Philippe works hard heading up our International Division. His slick tongue has been instrumental in convincing buyers at major stores to carry our brand and he's the entire reason our popularity has exploded in the Middle East. Our brand is especially popular among the billionaires of Dubai.

"Work hard but play hard, too. Everything won't come

crashing down if you pause for a little fun sometimes. You need to get laid. I don't know why you never take my advice."

Something on my face must change because his arm, in the process of raising his coffee cup to his mouth, pauses in mid-air.

"You ... took my advice? Don't take this the wrong way, dear brother, but it must not have been any good if you still look this pissed off."

That startles a laugh out of me. It feels good. I stand and stretch a little. Why am I confining myself behind this desk when I'm not getting any work done anyway?

"You remember that day you saw me dressed so strangely?"

His lip curls in distaste, clearly remembering the day he caught me sneaking back into our hotel room wearing those cheap clothes.

"I remember. Although I wish I didn't."

"Well, I met someone that day. Just a woman on the street. She threw her coffee on me."

Philippe narrows his eyes at me. "I would have thrown my coffee on that hideous shirt as well but I have to say, you are very odd if that is what turns you on."

I snatch the coffee cup from his hand. The assistant he hired makes way better coffee than mine. "Nothing happened. I just meant that I had fun. She had no idea who I was. She was actually annoyed with me. Annoyed. Can you imagine?"

He chuckles. "None of the women we know would dare express annoyance or any other real emotion. They're all hoping they tempt the famous Andre Lavin to put a ring on her finger and make her the reigning queen of the fashion world."

"It was refreshing to be out amongst regular people. People who don't want anything from me."

His expression softens and I have to turn away from the questions in his eyes. My brother is the person I'm closest to in the world but even he often doesn't understand me. The life we live suits him much better than me. He lives for the parties and the attention. It's always been a puzzle to him how I can crave success and be simultaneously frustrated as I achieve more of it.

Truthfully, I'm not entirely sure I understand it myself.

"Good. Maybe you should do that more often. If it helped last time, do it again. We're in the land of opportunity. Anything is possible here so why not reinvent yourself once more?" He glances over at me with a sly look. "But perhaps slightly better clothes this time."

I hand him back the now-empty cup. "That's actually a good idea. Finish reviewing those sketches for me, *per favore*?"

His mouth falls open as I start for the door. "What?

You're leaving? We have a meeting this afternoon. Those investors Mamma introduced us to at the gala are almost ready to sign on."

"I'm sure you can handle it. What was it you said? Everything won't come crashing down if I pause for a little fun sometimes?"

He looks murderous but clamps his lips closed.

Before I can get to the door, it opens and my assistant, Kate, pokes her head into the room. "The models are here."

I turn slowly to Philippe. "And I'm sure you can also approve the models for the next show."

He shakes his head. "You're seriously going to leave?"

Before I can walk out, a line of women passes by and I have to step back to allow them to enter. The last one pauses and squeals when she sees me.

"It's you! OMG!" She pronounces it phonetically. Oh-em-gee. "I'm such a *huge* fan of yours. I've been following you on Instagram since the beginning."

"Thank you for the support. Fans like you are what keep us in business."

It sounds like a line but it's the truth. No matter how tired or rushed I may be, I always take time out for fans who approach me in the street or at events. When I wasn't sure I was going to get seed capital to start my line, online fans were willing to donate money to help me get my start. Those same fans support each new launch and promote our brand tire- lessly for free. I am truly grateful.

"I hate to ask but can I have your autograph?" She blushes and glances over her shoulder to where everyone else is waiting.

"Of course." My hand pulls a pen from my top pocket automatically. I wait, expecting her to produce a napkin or a notepad. I've signed everything from menus to receipts.

Then she pulls down her top, exposing her shoulder and the majority of her left breast. "You can make it out to Katy with a Y. I can't wait to post this picture to Instagram."

My hand moves as quickly as possible, scrawling my name right under her collarbone. When I'm done, *Katy with a Y* giggles again, brushing her hand over my arm as she thanks me. She joins the other models, showing off my signature with a smirk.

Philippe raises a hand in a wave. "I've got this. Go do ... What are you going to do?"

"Hell if I know. I just have to get out of here."

As I'm leaving, Jason Gautier, the company COO and one of my best friends, enters carrying a suit in a garment bag. "Wait, where are you going?"

"I'm leaving early."

His eyes dart between me and Philippe. "Leaving early?"

Philippe looks amused. "Yes. He's leaving early. Taking some time for fun. I'm sure you're familiar with the concept."

Jason blinks. "Not really. When has he ever left early? Where is he even going?"

"To get coffee," I shout over my shoulder as I leave my brother and best friend arguing over my workaholic nature.

As I'm leaving, I hear his perplexed, "But you hate American coffee!"

After wandering aimlessly for almost an hour, I had to admit that my attempt at relaxation was a failure. Disgusted with myself, I finally just hailed a cab and went back to my hotel.

Only to discover that my mother was waiting for me to escort her to a charity dinner I never agreed to attend.

I grimace, hoping that I didn't offend anyone tonight. Considering my mood, I'm sure I was terrible company but I couldn't disappoint my mother. Although she pretends that nothing bothers her, I know she hates attending social functions alone. It's something she still isn't quite used to, even though my father has been gone five years now.

Now that I've done my duty for the night and Mamma is settled, I find myself at a loss. As I ride the elevator back down to the lobby, I ponder an entire night to do whatever I want. No thoughts of work and no one to answer to. The freedom is almost daunting.

The doorman tips his hat as I pass and I respond to a

friendly *hello* from one of the valets outside. I give him my ticket so he can bring my car around and then my attention lands on the other. He's a young man but old enough for what I need. Probably still in college considering that he doesn't look as though he's fully grown into his large hands and feet. His eyebrows lift as I walk closer.

"Good evening. I want to go out. On the town. To have fun." I force myself to stop talking, embarrassed by my own rambling.

The young man takes it in stride. Especially when I slide over a few twenties. He pockets the money and then points down the block. "There's a nightclub called *Hysteria* three streets over that's pretty popular. It's the place to be. Difficult to get into but worth it from what I hear."

I shake my head, already sure another exclusive club filled with rich people trying to impress each other is not what I want.

"No clubs. I don't want a popular place with a VIP lounge. I want to experience some real American fun. Something normal. Where would you go if you had the night off?"

He looks skeptical but nods his head in the other direction. "It's not that close; it's in Adams Morgan. A bar called *Hammered.* They have the best happy hour and every Friday it's half-priced wings. *All night.*"

"Excellent. That's where I'll go."

My enthusiasm seems to surprise him but he quickly

recovers. "It's a really fun place. They have pool and darts, too. But you can't go like that." He gestures to my suit. "It's ... not a dressy type of place."

I clap him on the back. "Oh, don't worry. I have just the thing to wear."

It doesn't take as long to put together the *normal guy* outfit this time. The white shirt is unsalvageable so I grab the next in the package, a plain, serviceable black. Despite the sad fabric, I can see a certain beauty to dressing this way. Without external adornment, the focus is completely on me. When I look in the mirror, it's like seeing myself for the first time after a long illness or being in a trance.

Like running into an old friend unexpectedly after years apart.

When I get downstairs I bypass the valets and go to the first cab idling at the curb. I looked up the bar online so I'd have the address handy. After I tell him my destination, the cab driver doesn't speak except to curse occasionally at other drivers. Which is fine by me. It gives me some time to gather my thoughts.

The bar is nestled between a barbecue eatery with a huge sign shaped like a pig and a music store. I pay the driver quickly and as soon as I exit the cab, I'm enveloped in a crowd of people walking along the sidewalk and chattering excitedly. Luckily they're going the same way I wanted to go and when they stop, I see that we're at *Hammered*.

I step into the slightly dim interior and take a moment to take it all in. There are several televisions hanging over the bar broadcasting a football game. I've never followed American football so I don't know the teams but when everyone in the bar lets out a rousing cheer, I find myself caught up in the excitement as well. A place opens up at the bar and I take a stool at the end.

"What'll ya have?" The bartender is dressed similarly, in jeans and a black shirt except his has the name of the bar on the breast pocket.

"I don't suppose you can do a Campari soda?" The look on his face tells me all I need to know. "Never mind. A beer. Whatever you recommend is fine."

I look around casually, taking in the general atmosphere and the people milling around in groups chatting. It's been years since I've been to a place like this. After university, Philippe and I used to enjoy going out with Jason who has radar for the hippest and hottest new nightspots.

When did things change? When did we stop having fun?

The bartender slides a beer down to me and I'm pleasantly surprised when I try it. He chuckles at the look on my face.

"It's our new summer ale. The owner brews it himself. It's

probably not the fancy stuff you're used to but ... "

I lean over the bar. "Fancy? What makes you think I'm used to fancy stuff?"

His eyebrow lifts. "Dude, you're wearing a Rolex in a bar."

As he leaves to tend to his other customers, I take my watch off and put it in my pocket. It's kind of funny. With all the work I put in to crafting a normal outfit, I completely missed the details. Maybe I should have called for backup.

I pull out my phone and dial Jason. He answers absently and slightly out of breath. The sounds of traffic filter through the line.

"Hey, are you busy right now?"

"Always busy," he responds automatically. "Why, what's up? We didn't have a meeting tonight did we?"

"No. The opposite. I'm attempting to relax. I could use some help."

He laughs. "Oh wow. First you leave early. Now you're actually going out. This I have to see. Wingman on the way."

Twenty minutes after I text him the name of the bar, he walks in still wearing a suit. He does a double take when he sees me.

"I'm so sorry, sir. I thought you were someone else. You remind me of my friend, Andre. But he would never be caught dead in cotton with anything less than 800 thread count."

I finger the T-shirt. "Maybe I'm trying something different."

"Philippe told me about your little experiment. I'm all for it."

"You are?" I ask, instantly suspicious.

He loves to tease me about being uptight but Jason has standards that are just as high as I do. I'm pretty sure he'd be physically ill if he couldn't eat at Michelin starred restaurants and have VIP access everywhere. He grew up poor and has resolved never to return to that life.

"Hell, yeah. Anything that gets you laid is a good idea." His eyes narrow. "So first, you probably should loosen up a bit. Lose the frown. No, don't smile like a clown. Just look relaxed. Like you're just hanging out."

I try out another expression but he still looks alarmed so I give up. "Let's just accept that this is my resting expression."

He blows out a breath. "Okay, so when you see a hot girl, don't talk about work, obviously. Ask her about herself, her job and whether she likes what she does. Chicks love that shit."

This seems like common sense to me so perhaps I'm worrying for nothing.

"Oh but make sure she knows you *have* a job. Tell her you own a company, just not which one. You don't want her to think you're a loser." He points at my shirt. "Maybe this is a bad idea. These clothes are like pussy repellent."

I take another swig of beer. "I can't talk about work but somehow I need her to know that I own my company. This is getting complicated."

Behind Jason's head, I see a swing of brown hair that looks familiar. I peer over his shoulder and then stand so I can see better.

The beautiful girl that threw her coffee on me yesterday morning is standing in the middle of the bar. The too-tight shirt is gone and instead she's wearing skintight jeans and a halter that shows off her shoulders and the sweet curve of her perky little breasts.

"Clumsy Girl. She's here," I say.

"Who?" Jason pauses with a beer halfway to his mouth.

She's walking toward us now. I whip around. The bar has filled up since I've been here and there are no more empty stools.

"You have to leave. Go, now!" I shove him off the stool right before she gets close. I barely hear Jason's muttered curse over the sound of my heart pounding.

She looks at the empty stool next to me and then around at the crowded bar.

That's right, beautiful. There are no other options.

After a brief pause, she glances over at me. "Is anyone sitting here?"

"No. Please, have a seat."

She climbs up and then places her small bag in her lap. When she looks over at me, I quickly look away.

"Hey, do I know you?"

I laugh softly. "Maybe if you bump into me and spill beer all over my shirt you'd remember."

Recognition lights her eyes and she smiles. "I knew you looked familiar. This is such an odd coincidence. But maybe this is a good sign for me. I think you're my lucky charm."

"Have I brought you luck, then?" I take the opportunity to stare at her and drink in my fill.

She's the kind of pretty that many people overlook. Brown hair and eyes but she has small, delicate features that give her an almost elvish appearance. Her lashes frame her eyes and give her a sexy, slumberous look despite how young she is. Like a good girl just waiting to go bad.

She shrugs but her cheeks flush pink at my close scrutiny. "When I met you yesterday–"

"You mean when you *accosted* me yesterday," I interrupt.

Her lips purse as she glares at me. It's so cute that it makes me want to annoy her just for the hell of it. That murderous expression on her innocent face is adorable. Like one of those tiny kittens that's convinced it's actually a fierce lion.

"Bumped into you. I *accidentally* bumped into you, and one could argue that you were at fault for just standing in the middle of the sidewalk like that."

I pretend to think about it. "I'm willing to accept a tiny part of the blame but I still lost a shirt in the process."

She winces. "Sorry about that. I'll pay for your dry cleaning."

"No need. It was part of a three-pack. Three shirts for the price of one. Fantastic."

"Okay then." She laughs. "Not sure I've ever met a guy so happy about a thrifty deal. But that's a good thing. Nothing wrong with saving money." She glances at my empty glass. "Can I buy you a drink?"

Shocked, I just stare at her for a second. "You want to buy me a drink?"

"Yes! I'm here celebrating and it's bad luck to toast with an empty glass. Or so I've heard."

There's no way she can know how rare it is for other people to buy me anything. Especially women. I'm used to picking up the check for my entire group of friends whenever we go out and the women I've dated expect flowers, jewelry and expensive gifts.

My lips curl up at this unexpected turn of events.

"I would love for you to buy me a drink. But it's probably best if I don't take a drink from a stranger. Andre." I hold out my hand.

She accepts it with a firm handshake. "I'm Casey. Nice to meet you. Again."

5

Casey

Two beers later, I'm still not sure what's happening. After buying him a drink, we talked about the city (we've both recently moved here) and my plans to finish my degree. I've never met a guy this attentive and easy to talk to and it's brought out a side of me that I've never felt before.

Who is this girl flirting with the sexiest guy in the bar?

Who is this siren confidently touching the back of his hand and flipping her hair as if she knows how to seduce someone?

I'm putting on a show but inside my inner dork is slowly melting down. What the hell am I doing? After dating one guy all through high school and then my fiasco with Thad the cheater in college, I don't exactly have a lot of experience. But isn't that the point of moving to the city and starting a whole new life? To do all the things I never got to do before, experience life and break out of my shell?

"So, I suppose it's a little late to be asking, but what are we celebrating?" He winks as he takes another sip of his beer.

His throat works as he swallows and I have to turn away, startled at my intense, visceral reaction to watching the muscles in his throat work. Heat creeps up my face and I have to work not to gawk at him like a teen girl with a crush.

"Actually the day I met you, I was on my way to a job interview. That's why I said you were a good luck charm. I got the job! Now, I'm here to check out whether I want to apply for a second job here. So seeing you is probably a good thing. Maybe it means I'll get hired here, too."

He raises his glass. "Well, let's toast to your new job. Congratulations. I hope it's the start of something great."

"I hope it's the start of something great, too. I could use some good news for a change." Not wanting to dwell on the crapstorm the last year has been, I smile and shake off all thoughts of the past. "Tell me more about you. What do you do?"

For the first time all night he looks wary. "I work in ... retail. Selling men's clothes."

That explains a lot actually, namely how he makes a

simple T-shirt and jeans look so damn good. Although I suspect the phenomenal genetics play a part in that, also.

"That must be fun."

"It can be," he says. "It can also be really demoralizing. Not that I'm complaining. I have a great life."

"You're not complaining, just being honest. Nobody has a perfect life. We all have good things and bad things we'd love to change."

"Yes, that's it exactly. I'm so grateful for the good things. And I love... clothes. So I'm truly happy with where I am."

"That's exactly what I want. In my career, I mean. Clearly I'm not talking about clothes. I'm not so good with clothes." I wave my hand over the worn jeans and halter I'm wearing. Ariana had warned me in advance that the bar was extremely casual, something I was grateful for. I didn't have that many dressy clothes.

"You look great," he shouts over the music. "Very comfortable."

That makes me chuckle. "Just what every girl wants to hear. Although you can get away with saying that in your accent. You could probably say 'hey, you look like shit' and it would sound elegant."

He laughs. "My family roots are French, Italian and some English that my mother refuses to admit to. But I've traveled so much in recent years that my accent has become a bit muddled."

"What was that again?" I lean over to hear what he just said. This bar is so loud but half of our communication has been flirty glances anyway. Plus, it gives me an excuse to lean closer to him.

His lids lower as I lean into his arm. My nipples tighten beneath the thin material of my halter top and I know he can tell. His sharp intake of breath proves it when I deliberately rub closer. Heat spreads from where his arm presses up against my breast.

For the next few years, I'm going to be focused on nothing but work. Climbing the corporate ladder and proving everybody back in Gracewell wrong. This is my last chance to let loose and actually have some fun before I'm committed to the life of a corporate drone.

Shouldn't I enjoy it while I have the chance?

I bite my lip, mulling it over. Part of me feels I should be ashamed considering going home with a guy when I don't even know his last name. But when I look at him, I don't feel like he's a stranger. Something about him puts me at ease and no man has ever made me feel so sexy.

Maybe I won't be having much fun over the next few years but at least I'll have one really great memory to carry me through all those long, lonely nights. Time stops when our eyes meet.

And I make a decision.

"The music has gotten really loud," I yell over the music. "Do you want to get out of here?"

His eyes hold mine, almost like he's trying to read between the lines. Taking a chance, I lean forward and brush my lips against his slightly. Before I can even pull back, he's got his finger up signaling for the bartender.

I open my small bag. After I bought him a drink we had another round (okay, two more rounds), so I'm sure our bill is really high by now. But before I can count out any money, he hands some bills to the bartender and holds out a hand to me.

The bar has gotten so crowded over the last two hours that we have to fight our way to the door to get out. When we finally step out onto the street, he entwines his fingers with mine.

"Don't want to lose you," he murmurs. He's so close that the sound of his deep voice next to my ear sends a shiver down my spine and straight between my legs. Jeez, this guy is like sex on a stick. Now that we're standing up I'm reminded of how tall he is and the muscles in his arms are straining the sleeves of his shirt in a way that makes my mouth water.

"We could find another place. Maybe get some coffee or find a restaurant and get something to eat. Something to soak up all the drinks."

I blink uncertainly. Did he not get my subtle hint back at the bar? Or is that not the way people proposition hot guys for sex? I'm clearly doing this wrong.

"Can I be honest?"

He nods and pulls me out of the flow of traffic until we're leaning up against the building. The noise recedes as we move a little away from the door of the bar.

"With my new job, I'm going to be really busy after this. I'm not looking for anything serious. But I'm really attracted to you. I've never felt like this with a guy before. So I guess what I'm saying is, I'd love to go look for a restaurant but I'd really rather go find a bed."

When he doesn't say anything, I swallow nervously. "Sorry. Maybe I misread things."

His eyes flash and he tugs me up on my toes. Our mouths crash together and his groan reverberates between our lips. All I can do is clutch his shirt, my fingers twisting in the material helplessly as he kisses me until I can't breathe.

When we finally break apart, we're both panting for air and I can feel how hard he is in his jeans.

"You didn't misread anything. And if it's okay with you, I'd love it if you'd come have a drink with me. In my hotel room."

I smile so hard that I want to cover it with my hands, sure I look like a crazy person. "Okay. Yes. Let's do that."

He pulls out his phone. "Let me just call us a car."

I nod. "That's one of the things I've loved since moving. We didn't have Uber where I come from. It's a small town."

He looks confused for a second but then nods. "Right.

Uber. Just one moment."

I can't see his screen but it feels like he's pushing way too many buttons to be using the Uber app. When he feels my eyes on him, he shrugs apologetically.

"Sorry, just telling my assistant not to bother me for the rest of the night. I want to focus on you."

Oh my god.

The thought of an entire night with him makes me squirm.

His eyes follow the movement of my hips and he curses suddenly. "You keep looking at me like that and I'm going to start undressing you on the street."

I cross my legs slightly trying to tame the ache that's suddenly throbbing between my thighs. He grabs my hand and tugs me toward the curb. He waves his arm in the air and a passing taxicab pulls over a few feet away.

"We're taking a cab. Waiting around is just wasting time." He holds the door open for me. "And Casey, the things I'm going to do to you are going to take time. A good, long time."

I really hope this doesn't turn out to be a mistake.

The entire cab ride, I keep my eyes fixed out the window, watching the sights speed by while we're on the way to... oh god, where are we even going?

This is like *Being Single 101*. Don't go somewhere alone with a guy if no one knows where you are. I discreetly pull my phone from my bag. I'll just text Ariana where I am when we arrive. She'll understand. And she's definitely not the type to judge.

Once the cab stops I quickly text Ari before climbing out. Holy crap, this is a nice hotel.

"Wow. This is a fancy place. You're staying here?"

It's hard not to gawk as we walk through the lobby. And I'm seriously questioning my decision to wear a halter top tonight. Why didn't I wear something nicer than this?

"My job pays for it. It's a great perk."

"This is definitely a great perk. You must be one hell of a salesman."

We enter the elevator and I'm pushed closer to him as another couple gets on. When I feel his arm wrap around me, I let my head fall to his chest briefly. A few floors later, we're alone in the elevator. It takes a few minutes for me to realize what's wrong. I laugh when I look at the elevator panel. None of the buttons are lit up.

"You forgot to push a button. What floor are you on?"

"Third floor."

I push the button and the elevator descends. It doesn't take long to reach his floor and I exit first, sending him a playful look over my shoulder. "I can't wait to see this room. If the rest of the hotel is any indication, I bet it's pretty swank."

He stops next to a room and pulls out his phone. I'm trying to pretend like this is all totally normal to me but inside all I'm thinking is, *Wow this hotel doesn't even use regular keycards?*

He holds the door open for me. "Does it meet with your approval?"

I put my bag down on the table next to the bed. The room is beautiful with gorgeous paintings on the wall and a balcony. But I'm not even looking at any of that. All of my attention is on the huge bed that looms in front of us. Suddenly I'm not so sure about this bold plan of mine.

What was I thinking?

I've never propositioned anyone in my life and I had to start with a guy who looks like he's invented a few sexual positions?

I sit on the edge of the bed, folding my hands in my lap.

"Would you like a drink?" He gestures toward the small minibar. "I'm not sure what's here but they usually have a pretty good selection."

Oh good. If we have a drink that gives me some time to loosen up a bit. "Sure. Maybe a glass of wine?"

He turns his back to me and starts rummaging on the bar. I use the opportunity to watch him when he's not looking. Tall and thin, he has the kind of compact frame common among runners or surfers. His dark hair is artfully tousled and I wonder if he's ever had a bad hair day.

Seriously, what the hell am I doing here with a guy who looks like he belongs in a Hugo Boss ad?

He turns and hands me a glass. I take a tentative sip, relaxing when I recognize it as champagne. I look up to find him watching me. "I guess you can tell I really don't do this often."

"Would you believe me if I told you I don't either? It's not that easy to trust people these days. I spend a lot of my free time on my own."

"Me too! I can't afford to get distracted. I trusted the wrong person in the past and had to drop out of school. Now I'm focused on my career. I really want to prove to myself that I can do this."

He nods his head. "I understand. Can I tell you a secret?"

"You can tell me anything. This is a one-night stand, remember? One night of fun before we go back to our real lives. We'll never see each other again so you can think of me like a vault. Whatever you tell me will never see the light of day."

"I want to do something completely different. I love what I do now but I also want to work on helping the less fortunate. Maybe a non-profit program to help them get warm clothes in the winter. Something like that."

I bump my shoulder against his. "I knew it. You're a good guy. I could tell."

His cheeks redden. "It's probably not going to happen.

There's a lot of people depending on me. For money, I mean. I need to focus on what's most profitable. I don't want to let them down."

"I understand that. My mom has always struggled and now that I have a new job, I'm going to be able to send money home to help her. So I get it. But that doesn't mean that you can't do this new project, too. If this is what you're meant to do, I think you'll find a way to balance the need to make a profit with your need to help others."

"You really think I can do that?"

Why does he seem so shocked that someone could believe in him? It makes me a little sad to think he doesn't have a cheerleader in his current circle of friends and family. I'm not sure if I could handle all the crazy stuff life has thrown at me recently if I didn't have my mom in my corner telling me she knows I can handle anything.

"Yes, I really think you can do it. Something tells me you can do just about anything."

When he notices I'm done with the champagne, he takes my glass. I slip my shoes off and tuck my legs underneath me. "This really is a beautiful room."

When I look up, he's watching me with that intense, sexy look.

Screw this. We're both adults and we know why we're here. I grab the front of his shirt, pulling him down on top of me. I can feel his shock, he's as stiff as a board at first but then he's lowering himself on top of me and our tongues are entwined.

It's so easy to get lost in his kiss but I know what I want and it doesn't involve him wearing this many clothes. Things are a mad scramble as we both pull off our clothes but finally we're naked and I've never felt anything better.

His mouth latches on to my breast, taking as much of it into his mouth as possible.

"Oh my god, I can't breathe." I gasp, overwhelmed by the sensation. My hips move restlessly, trying to get the contact I need. But he's not moving with me, holding himself still as if he's trying not to frighten me.

"Don't tease me. Please."

He growls, a low rumbling sound that makes me tighten internally, imagining this magnificent male animal taking me. He reaches over the side of the bed for his pants, coming back with a condom. It's an embarrassing but educational moment to watch him roll it down his considerable length.

He pauses, looking unsure now that we're both naked and things are about to go down. I touch his face gently. "This is just going to be one night, right? One last night of fun before I have to be all boring and serious."

"One night," he agrees. "But if one night is all we have, then I'd better make it count."

I wrap my arms around his shoulders. "You're damn straight. Show me what you've got."

6

Andre

Something tickles my nose and I open my eyes. Sunlight streams through the curtains I forgot to close last night. Drapes were definitely the last thing on my mind when we stumbled into this room.

I blink sleepily and peer around the unfamiliar room. Kate is a miracle worker. Seriously, best assistant ever. Who else could I call and ask for a new hotel room and have the digital key on my app less than ten minutes later? Amazing.

Not sure what miracle she pulled off to have a room ready for me that fast but I don't care. All I care about is the results. There was no way I could bring Casey up to the Presidential

Suite after spending so much effort to get her to see me as a regular guy.

And she did. She knows nothing of what I do for a living or about the money or the fame. To her, I'm just a guy with slightly bad fashion sense who seems to bump into her a lot. And yet, she likes me anyway.

My chest warms when I think about her and that's when it hits me. My head whips to the right, the space where Casey should be.

The space that contains nothing but rumpled sheets and a pillow.

Suddenly wide awake, I sit straight up and kick the blanket off. I'm still naked but I don't care about that as I walk over to the bathroom and knock on the door. When I open it, it's empty. Heart pumping now, I run to the door of the room and step out into the hall.

"Oh my!"

There's a middle-aged couple in the hall pushing a baby in a stroller. The mother covers her mouth in surprise but her eyes drop to my dick swinging in the wind. The father scowls at me and then puts his hand over his wife's eyes.

"Sorry." I close the door and lean back against it. There's no way around it.

Casey left.

Perplexed, I stalk around the room staring at the rumpled bed linens as if they can give me the answers. Did I do something to scare her away? It's not bragging to say that I've never had a woman run out on me before. Usually, morning afters consist of round four or five of sex followed by a leisurely brunch.

Then I'm usually the one trying to find a tactful way to escape.

But this ... I don't know what to make of this. She ditched me! The more I think about it, the more absurd it seems. As I'm pacing, my foot runs over something and I lean down to pick it up. My blood heats when I see what it is. The panties I peeled off Casey last night.

I chuckle, only now able to see the design on the cotton. Purple and pink unicorns cover the fabric. As pissed off as I am, I can't help laughing. Only Casey could wear such unsexy panties and still have me panting for more. Maybe it's a metaphor for this whole situation. She's like this mythical creature that I've only dreamed up. Hell, maybe I had one too many beers last night and the whole thing was a dream.

Then I'm hit with a visceral memory of her tight, wet heat as I slid inside her, the way she moaned in my ear and shuddered beneath me every time she came.

That wasn't a dream. It was the best damn sex I've ever had. And instead of enjoying more of it, I'm standing in the middle of a basic hotel room with a stiff dick holding the most ridiculous panties I've ever seen.

My phone is still on the nightstand where I put it last

night. I'm checking for messages when it hits me. We never exchanged numbers. I don't even think I got her last name. I look over at her side of the bed again and that's when I see the note propped up on the other nightstand. I crawl over the bed and snatch it eagerly. It's just two lines scrawled on the hotel stationery.

Last night was amazing.

You really are my lucky charm.

I stare at the paper in disbelief. That's it? Just two lines and she didn't even sign her name?

Then I see that she's written something on the outside. When I peer closer what I see scrawled there only makes me feel worse.

No, what I see written there makes my blood boil.

"Who the fuck is *Andrew?*"

"Okay, the investigator got nothing."

Jason sits on the edge of my desk as he delivers the bad news. Not that I didn't know it was coming.

"Our social media team tried to find her on Facebook, Twitter and Instagram. I'm at a loss as to what to do next. I'm this close to calling my ex-girlfriend and asking for her help. No one can stalk someone like her. Trust me. I know this from experience."

It's been a week and I've tried everything. I waited in the lobby of the hotel that morning hoping she might come back. After that I called ASI, the private security firm we've been using while in the States. The owner, Elliott Alexander, took the case personally after his employees failed to find anything. He tried the name Casey, spelled with both a K and a C. He tried the initials K.C.

Eventually he concluded that without a last name, or certainty that I even have the correct *first* name, it would be virtually impossible to find her.

That's when I went on the hunt.

I went back to the bar where we had drinks that night and asked around. That just got me thrown out. Apparently asking about a girl when you don't know her last name or anything else about her other than what her pussy tastes like is considered creepy.

Then I went to the coffee shop where we first met and got nothing for my trouble other than a few more bad lattes. The girl behind the counter kept looking at me like I was a serial killer when I tried to describe Casey. To be fair, it's hard to describe a sexy woman without sounding like a pervert. If I can't mention her round ass and perky tits then all I'm left with is brown hair, brown eyes and the ability to make me laugh. A smile that makes me feel warm inside. A kiss that turns me on and also makes me want to protect her.

None of those things have been helpful in identifying her.

And each day, I'm losing hope. The facts are in my face and have been getting clearer by the day. Casey either doesn't exist or she doesn't want to be found.

I'm not sure which I find more alarming.

Jason sighs. "I get that this is frustrating but it's just one girl. Hell, I'll go with you back to the bar and we can find another one."

"I don't want another one," I mutter petulantly. "I want that one. You don't get it. This girl is special."

"Her pussy was special." At my glare, he holds his hands up. "Not trying to piss you off. I'm just saying. You wanted to get laid. You got laid. Now it's time to move on."

"Maybe you're right. If I can't find her that has to mean something."

"It does mean something. Clearly it was meant to be a one-time deal. Maybe Casey was just dumped and wanted to have some revenge sex to make herself feel better. Maybe she's a bored housewife who was using you for a thrill while her husband was away on business. Hell, maybe that's not even her name and she's actually an undercover agent with the FBI. Does it really matter? It wasn't like you really knew her, right?"

His words poke at a sore spot inside that I don't want to examine too closely. Everything he's saying is correct. We spent most of our time talking in a loud, crowded bar and then the rest of it sliding our tongues over each other's skin.

Can I really pretend that what we had was some deep, spiritual connection? She didn't even get my name right. I can blame that one on the crowded bar, but it's probably a little crazy that I'm this upset over the way our night together ended and she doesn't even know my name.

It shouldn't bother me so much but it does.

Jason stands. "You had a great time and now it's over. Count yourself as lucky. Most guys have trouble getting rid of their one-night stands. Yours did the hard work for you."

After he leaves, I sit for a while taking things in. I've been an asshole to everyone for the past week and I'm sure Jason drew the short straw on who would come in here and have a talk with me. This is a critical time for my company. We're expanding from menswear and working to make ourselves a complete brand that sells everything for men and women, including accessories and even perfume. If there's ever been a worse time for me to have my head out of the game, I can't think of it.

I have to let it go.

7

Casey

Two months later...

"I am not having this conversation."

I pick up my headset, completely prepared to ignore the inappropriate conversation happening behind me. I've been working as a receptionist at Mirage Advertising for two months now and as cheesy as it is, I feel I've finally found home. I can wear business-casual attire, I have plenty of free time to do the assigned reading for my online classes and the office manager, Anya Petrova, is quickly becoming my best friend. Even though she loves to make me really uncomfortable.

"Why not?" Anya puts a piece of paper down on the copier tucked in the corner behind me. "Seriously, I miss sex. Don't you? When was the last time you got laid?"

"You want an exact date?"

She rolls her eyes. "That tells me you don't remember. Which is a problem. We need to go out this weekend."

"The only place I'll be going this weekend is the refrigerator for more ice cream, not to some bar to pick up strangers. I'm staying away from men remember? It's kept me out of trouble so far." I adjust my headset and pull my chair closer to the desk.

Anything to distract myself from thoughts that it wasn't too long ago that I got really up close and personal with a stranger.

And it was definitely trouble.

"Who said anything about a stranger? Friends with benefits is a thing for a reason." Anya pushes another button on the copy machine. A second later there's a crunching sound and a piece of paper shoots out wrinkled and torn.

"Damn this place! I told Law we need a new copy machine." Anya grabs the sheet of paper and crumples it into a ball before throwing it in the recycle bin. "That man can't see what's right in front of his face."

I wisely choose not to comment. Anya has a not-so-secret

crush on our boss, James Lawson, which causes her no end of frustration.

"Friends with benefits only works if you have friends. I'm not exactly Miss Popular."

I've always been something of a loner but since moving to the city it's been even harder to meet new people. Sure, I could probably hang out with my roommate Ariana but I don't want to wear out my welcome. It isn't that she hasn't been nice to me; she has. But I sometimes get a vibe that she's not interested in hanging out or getting too close with me.

Plus, to be honest that girl is into some weird stuff. I cringe just thinking about some of the things I've come across by accident in the apartment.

Let's just say I'll never borrow clothes from Ari again.

"You haven't met *anyone* since you've moved here?" Anya shakes her head like she can't understand the concept. "Not even a hot neighbor walking his dog or something?"

The way she says it makes me feel like even more of a loser. Most of my neighbors work long hours. I only see them in passing as they come to and from work. The people I see at the grocery store and on the subway seem to change daily.

It's such a stark contrast to Gracewell, where everyone knows each other and crime is almost nonexistent. The entire atmosphere of city life is different. My first week on the job, I thought everyone was talking to themselves until I realized they all had little Bluetooth earpieces in. Some of the women in the office even wear them in the bathroom. I can't think of anyone I want to talk to *that* badly.

It's no wonder I have trouble fitting in.

Anya puts something on the desk in front of me. It's an internal memo for the Preview Gala, a company event that showcases the agency's best design work for the past year and introduces our newest campaigns. It's all the marketing executives have been talking about for the past few weeks.

"The Preview Gala is the perfect opportunity for you to meet people. Obviously Law doesn't want us dating current clients but lots of our past clients come and they're fair game. This will be a good chance for you to network. You know, now that you're working with the marketing team."

Recently, I've been given some marketing duties in the afternoon while Anya covers the phones. I still can't believe it. This is the kind of chance I didn't think I'd get until after I graduated. I'll get to work on some interesting projects and gain experience for my résumé. It also gives me a break from the tedium of being stuck behind the reception desk.

"I'm really excited about it. This is the first time I'll actually get to use some of the stuff we're learning in school. Hopefully I don't screw up too badly."

Anya waves that away. "Don't worry. Mya is so cool to work with. I assisted her a few times before I got promoted to office manager."

Mya is married to one of the other team leaders, Milo

Hamilton. Tall with piercing blue eyes, he looks more like a model than an advertising executive, something that seems pretty common around here. I fidget and adjust the buttons on my new blouse. Since so many of my clothes didn't fit properly, I was forced to pony up the dough for some new ones. But sitting at the reception desk gives me a front-row seat to what everyone else is wearing. What worked in Gracewell definitely doesn't cut it here.

I need to step it up.

An hour later, it's time for lunch so Anya comes back to relieve me. As I'm getting ready to leave, Mya stops by.

"Hey, Casey. I know we were supposed to start you on our next project but I think we should postpone it. I don't want to throw you into the deep end right away and the client that's coming in tomorrow is a little … difficult."

"*An asshole,*" Anya mutters behind us.

When Mya turns to look at her, Anya drops her eyes back to her computer screen. "Figured I'd say what we're all thinking."

Mya sighs. "She's right. This guy is not an easy client to deal with so usually Milo and I handle him together and leave the rest of the team out of it. There's no reason we should all feel like shit."

"That bad, huh?"

"Unfortunately, yes. He wasn't always like this which makes it so weird. He's a fashion designer so maybe it's to be expected. Aren't they always super demanding with diva-sized egos?"

I can't pretend I'm not a little scared to start with a client from hell, but one of the major points of working with the marketing executives is to find out if I have what it takes to work in the industry. Watching how two seasoned professionals deal with a tough situation is valuable experience for me.

"If you don't mind me being there, I'd still really like to help. I'm sure watching how you and Mr. Hamilton deal with a difficult client will be a great learning experience for me."

Mya nods once. "Good point. I'm impressed. After lunch, I'll bring you up to speed and give you some notes to review before tomorrow's meeting. If you keep this up, you might be working here on our marketing team one day."

Once Mya walks away, Anya gives me a thumbs up.

"Did you hear that? Or did I just hallucinate?" The idea that I might actually get hired on the marketing team is too much for me to handle. Mirage is an exclusive agency. They only handle high-end clients, usually Fortune 500 companies and celebrities. This is not the kind of place where you get hired straight out of school unless you're Ivy League.

"I heard that." Anya holds up her palm for a high five. "You've got this in the bag."

"Not quite." I bite my lip. "But what I have is a chance. As long as I don't do anything to screw it up, which is a real concern. I have a long history of screwing up at the worst possible moment. And if this client is as bad as she thinks … ?"

"He is. I'm not going to lie. But there's one good thing about the client from hell. He's grade A eye candy. Seriously. You need to have a drool rag handy."

"That good, huh? I thought you had your eye on a certain someone else."

Anya purses her lips. "Maybe I do. Maybe I don't. But that doesn't mean my eyes don't work. You'd have to be dead not to lust after Mr. Lavin. Trust me, you'll understand once you see him. Just try not to make eye contact or you might turn to stone."

I take a deep breath. I can do this. First, I'll get lunch and then I'll come back refreshed and ready to go. Once Mya gives me some notes to review about the client, I can spend this evening studying up.

Nothing is going to ruin this for me. Especially not some random asshole.

The afternoon passes quickly and by the time five o'clock rolls around, I'm worried my brain is going to explode. Mya is so patient and explains any marketing terms that I'm unfamiliar with but even with her help, it's obvious that I'm completely out of my depth.

Not that I thought this job would be a cakewalk but I definitely thought the marketing classes I'd already taken would have given me more to work with. Instead all I've discovered today is how much more I need to learn.

I trudge up the stairs to my apartment, ignoring the slight burn in my thighs. Ever since I moved in, I've been determined to keep using the stairs. At least I can make it without feeling like I need an oxygen tank now.

When I walk in, Ariana looks up from her perch on the couch and smiles politely. Oreo barks at the sight of me and then goes back to sniffing her butt.

Yup, that's about how welcome I feel around here.

"Hey there. You're home early."

Ariana shrugs and then clicks another button on the remote. "I changed shifts with another nurse."

She doesn't volunteer any other information and I take that as a hint not to ask. At first, she was a lot more welcoming and seemed like she'd be a cool new friend. But over the past few weeks, she's withdrawn a lot and I'm starting to wonder if she regrets allowing me to move in. Especially since she only did it as a favor to Mya, who was her previous roommate and her best friend.

I'm sure living with me is nowhere near as much fun as living with her bestie.

"Do you want me to move out?" I blurt before I can debate the wisdom of poking a sleeping bear.

Ariana looks up in surprise. "What?"

Well, it's already out there now so there's no point in trying to walk it back. Maybe clearing the air will make things less tense around here.

"You seemed really friendly when I first got here but then less so over the last few weeks. If you're regretting letting me move in, I'd rather know so I'll have time to find something better than that scary motel I was staying in before."

Ariana smiles, a genuine smile this time. "You don't hold back. I respect that. Sorry if I've been a little bitchy."

"You haven't. Not really. But I feel bad that you're not charging me market value for the room. You're not even getting a profit for your trouble."

"The money doesn't matter. I wanted a roommate so I wouldn't have to come home to an empty apartment all the time."

That's when it hits me.

"You miss her."

Ari doesn't look at me as she continues changing the channel on the television. "Yeah. But she's happy so that's what matters."

Now I really feel insensitive. Of course she's not warming up to me; she went from having her best friend around all the time to living with some random girl from nowheresville.

"You're a good friend."

Ari scoffs. "Not really. I'm just trying not to be that

jealous bitch who begrudges her friend's happiness. Anyway, what's your deal? All I've seen you do since you moved in is work and sleep. Haven't seen you with any guys or anything."

The question shouldn't surprise me considering how blunt Ariana usually is, but for some reason it takes me completely off guard. Probably because of the conversation I had with Anya today. It has me thinking about things I shouldn't be, things that are much better left in the past.

"Are you blushing? Woo, does that mean you've been sneaking a guy in here while I've been busy feeling sorry for myself?"

"There's been no sneaking," I splutter, then put my hands on my cheeks, feeling the heat there. "I told you I don't have a boyfriend."

"Mm-hmm. But there's one you want."

"One I can't have," I mutter under my breath.

Ari sighs. "I can relate."

While I sit, stunned at the thought that a girl who looks like a supermodel can relate, Ari puts the remote down. "I'm going to order pizza." She picks up Oreo, who looks annoyed to have her evening lick fest interrupted, and walks into the kitchen.

Now that we've broken the ice, we chat easily while we wait for the pizza. Ariana seems to be in a much better mood and flirts with the teenage pizza delivery boy, sending him away with a wink and a hefty cash tip. I can only shake my head at his perplexed but awed look. Ariana in flirt mode is probably more than most grown men would be able to handle.

After a few slices of pizza, I pull up my homework on my phone and do the reading for my class while giving Oreo the belly scratches she demands. Eventually Ari goes to her room and closes the door.

I blink at my phone when I see the time, then stand and stretch. I've been reading for more than an hour still wearing my work clothes. It's definitely time to change into something comfortable before I attempt to tackle the rest of the client notes Mya gave me this afternoon.

In my room, I drop my oversized bag on the bed and unbutton my blouse. Since I've been here, I have covered the bed with a purple comforter and stacked the bed with pillows. The furniture Mya left behind is good quality so I haven't felt the need to do much other than put up some pictures.

My thoughts drift back to my earlier conversation with Ariana. This is a nice room, very homey. But it's *not* home. Ari doesn't talk much about her family so I'm not sure where they are or if this apartment is the only home she has.

At that thought, I pull my phone from my bag and hit the first speed dial. I tuck my phone into the curve of my shoulder so I can rummage through the dresser for some pajama pants.

My mother works the night shift at the Gracewell retirement home because the later shift brings in more money.

Since I don't feel comfortable making personal calls during work hours, I've gotten into the routine of calling her at night before bed. By then most of the seniors have everything they need for the night and my mom is able to take a break and chat.

"Hi, sweetie. How are you?" She sounds upbeat but I can hear the exhaustion in my mother's voice.

"I'm great, Mom. In fact, I got a small promotion at work. I'll actually be working with the marketing team now instead of just sitting behind the front desk."

"I knew it! Didn't I tell you? Anybody can see what a hard worker you are and how smart you are. I'll just bet they promote you again once you finish your degree. I'm so proud of you." Mom sighs, the sound filled with contentment.

My mother never criticizes me or makes me feel guilty but I know her life would have been completely different if she hadn't gotten pregnant and had to drop out of college. She works so hard all the time but never complains. The only time I've ever heard her cry is when I called to tell her I was dropping out of school. It feels good to give my mom a reason to smile again.

"I hope so. Maybe one day I'll be on the marketing team and finally be able to help you out with the bills some."

"Cassandra Anne, I am just fine. I told you I make more working the late shift at this place. They gave me a nice increase to steal me away from the hospital. They have a hard time finding nurses with the patience to deal with some of the older folks here. They can get a little ornery sometimes. I just want you to concentrate on your studies. I don't need anything."

"I know but you shouldn't have to work so hard all the time. You deserve a break. Or at least to go back to the normal shift again."

"But I don't want to change shifts, baby girl. I've gotten used to this schedule and well, I have friends here."

I grin. My mom almost sounds *embarrassed.* "Mom, do you have a boyfriend at work? Is it one of the other night nurses?"

"Now, I didn't say anything like that. I just enjoy my work, that's all. They need me here at night. Another nurse might not understand why Mr. Jansen likes his dinner plate arranged a certain way or why Mrs. Hodges wears pink bunny slippers to bed."

"I'm glad you're enjoying it, Mom. I just want to make sure you're not running yourself into the ground."

"Casey, stop worrying about me so much. Worrying is supposed to be my job. Well, I should probably get back to work now. Keep up the good work, sweetie. Love you."

"Love you, too." I toss my cell phone in the middle of my bed. Growing up, my mom worked such odd hours and sometimes multiple jobs to make ends meet. I'm going to send her money whether she wants it or not but it's nice to know her latest job is making her happy at least.

I flop down on my bed and pull the client folder from my bag. Tomorrow is a big day and considering what a jerk this client is supposed to be, I want to be prepared. Not that I think I'll learn anything Mya doesn't already know but at least I won't ask any stupid questions. I prop the folder open in my lap and start reading.

My eyes drift closed before I finish the first page.

8

Andre

I push through the revolving door and into the lobby of the Madison building. Jason is already in the waiting area talking on his phone. Philippe should have been here already, too. I glance at my watch and then scowl at the time.

This is our third meeting with our marketing agency in the last month and I have no confidence this one will go any better than the last two.

Not that I can voice that opinion. Apparently I've been difficult to work with lately so anything I say will be taken negatively.

Kate rushes into the lobby looking harried. "Mr. Lavin! You're here early." She gives Jason a hard look before pulling out her phone.

I don't respond, unsure why being early requires a warning.

Jason shrugs. "I was trying to call you. Our last meeting ended early. Hopefully James can accommodate us."

"Of course! I'm sure it's fine." Her voice is upbeat but her fingers fly over the screen of her phone frantically.

Who could she be texting right now when we have a meeting to attend?

Jason leans over. "She's probably warning everyone upstairs that the dragon has left his lair." He chuckles when Kate glares at him.

I hit the button for the elevator. The past month has been a test of my patience in every way. Although I originally planned to stay in the States during this brand transition, last week I made the decision to go back to Milan for the duration. Why stay in a concrete prison enduring rain and questionable air quality when I could be at home, enjoying the exceptional weather and exquisite food?

"I'm ready to get this meeting done. We have a schedule to keep," I grumble, already irritated. We're flying back to Italy in just a few hours and another pointless meeting is not how I want to spend my time before getting on a plane.

Jason clears his throat before glancing at me. "So, before we attend this meeting maybe we should nail down what we hope to accomplish today. The last couple of meetings have been a little chaotic."

"Meaning that I've hated everything they've come up with." I adjust my tie slightly in the mirror image on the elevator doors.

He shifts next to me. "Meaning that you've made up your mind to hate everything because you've been in a shitty mood for what feels like six months straight."

My hand pauses on my tie.

After Jason broke the news that the investigators couldn't find Casey, I thought I'd come to terms with it. But even after I called off the official investigation, she was never far from my thoughts. I couldn't stop thinking about her at the most random moments and my lack of focus did not go unnoticed.

So I threw myself into my work with a vengeance, staying later at the office and coming in earlier. Maybe I was subconsciously punishing myself for allowing the most captivating woman I've ever met to slip through my fingers or maybe I truly thought that work could help me forget. But that time, Philippe was the one given the task of telling me that several of my staff members were on the verge of quitting.

Now I've reached a point where I have to accept that this isn't something I can fix. No amount of hard work or dedication will right this situation.

"You're right. I haven't been myself."

Jason looks stunned at my agreement but just then the elevator doors slide open. The head of the agency is waiting there to greet us, with the two lead marketing executives who have been working on our account standing directly behind him. Mya Taylor and Milo Hamilton worked together on the campaign that launched Lavin Bridal into a very successful year. Approving the campaign for that launch wasn't nearly so difficult and I can concede that it was entirely due to my state of mind.

Clumsy Girl is gone, as surely as if she was just a figment of my imagination. I've heard it from everyone over the last month: Jason, my brother and even the bartender at the bar I can't seem to stay away from.

She's gone.

It sucks the way things ended but I have to accept that it did end. Casey and I had a brief, magical moment and it changed me.

Maybe that's all it was meant to do.

I extend my hand. "James, I apologize for arriving so early. I hope we haven't inconvenienced you too greatly."

He shakes my hand and then motions to the others. "It's no problem at all. The team has put together a fantastic presentation for you today."

As he's speaking, my eyes are drawn to the reception desk behind him. A young woman stands and then when she notices me, freezes. But she's not the one I'm looking at. No, all of my attention is on the young woman sitting behind the desk, her attention fixed on her computer. She's wearing some type of headset and her dark hair is twisted up into a bun. But there's no mistaking that face.

That adorable, frustrating face.

Clumsy Girl is here.

My feet move forward without my permission as I walk away from James, leaving Jason and Kate to continue with the pleasantries. I'm definitely being rude but that's something I'll have to deal with later. After looking for her so long, maybe this is where I finally crack. Hell, the woman I'm staring at is probably a sixty-year-old grandmother and my mind is simply superimposing the image I've longed to see.

Then she looks up and sees me. Her face freezes into a mask of horror. After a few seconds where we stare at each other in mutual disbelief, she murmurs something to the woman next to her.

And that's when I get angry.

"James, please introduce me to your new receptionist. I don't think I've had the pleasure."

Everyone stills at my command. Or maybe because my voice feels abnormally loud. I clear my throat and smooth my tie, mainly to keep my hands busy so they don't reach out and grab the woman staring back at me defiantly from behind the desk.

"Of course. Mr. Lavin, this is Cassandra Michaels. She's been here with us for about two months and has been a great asset to the team."

While he talks I hold Casey's gaze, delighted by how her cheeks flush red under the praise. She darts a glance over at me and then does an awkward half wave, as if I'll settle for that. But I've spent the last two months searching for her after she gave me a fake name so I'm not letting her off that easily.

I approach the reception desk with my hand outstretched, knowing that she'll have to get up and shake it or appear rude.

She swallows, the sound audible. But she stands and walks around the desk. Or at least, she tries to. However, it appears she's forgotten that her headset is connected to the computer so as she walks away, the cord yanks her back and she lands sprawled on the floor.

Staring right up between my legs.

"Kill me now."

Her voice was barely above a whisper but everyone else must have heard it too because I hear choking sounds behind me that can only be laughter.

"Are you okay, Casey?" James appears at my elbow with a hand outstretched to help her up. But there's no way he's touching her before I do. So I lean down and extend a hand. She looks hesitant but finally takes it.

"I'm so sorry, sir."

Hearing her call me that takes me from shock to outrage.

Sir? Like I'm some stranger she's meeting for the first time? I have a sudden overwhelming urge to remind her just how well we know each other but the pleading look in her eyes stops me.

"Please. Don't get me fired," she whispers, turning her head away slightly so James can't hear.

"There is nothing to be sorry for," I say loud enough for everyone to hear.

Then I bring her hand to my mouth and dust a kiss over her knuckles. The gesture will look polite to anyone watching but Casey sucks in a sudden breath.

James and the others have already started talking amongst themselves about the meeting. No one is paying attention to us right now. They don't feel the heat being generated right at their feet.

"I can't say the sight of you in any position is something to apologize for," I finish in a voice for her alone.

When she sees that no one is looking anymore, Casey rips her hand from mine. "What are you doing here?"

"I have a meeting," I reply, knowing the casual response will annoy her. But who can blame me for wanting to see those honey eyes light up with fire again? I've seen just how passionate she can get, after all.

She pulls off her headset with a frustrated huff. "Look, what happened between us ... We should just forget about it. Right? We can do that."

"What am I supposed to forget exactly? How much fun we had talking in the bar that night? Or that we spent hours bringing each other pleasure? That I've never felt anything like that with another woman? Which part is supposed to be so forgettable?"

My bold statement is met with a glare before she plasters on a wide smile. "Of course, Mr. Lavin. It was so nice to meet you, too!"

When I turn, I catch Jason's eye. He's staring at Casey but I don't think he's recognized her yet.

The others have started walking toward the hallway that leads to the conference room. I can't stay here too much longer without drawing undue attention which is exactly what Casey has asked me not to do.

Her eyes turn pleading. *"Please, don't make a scene. I need this job."*

As angry as I am, I can't ignore the desperation in her voice. She told me that night at the bar she was celebrating getting a new job, one she was very excited and grateful for. No matter how pissed I was to wake up alone, I wouldn't want to take that from her.

"I won't say anything."

Her shoulders drop in relief and she lets out a sigh that reminds me a little too much of the sounds she made that night in my arms. It definitely pricks at my ego that she seems to have no problem moving on from the night we shared when

I've been haunted by it ever since. Could it be possible that the night that was life changing for me was only average for her?

Then our eyes meet again and she shivers. Heat explodes between us and I have to clench my hands into fists to keep from reaching out for her. No, she feels this, too. But wants to deny it for some reason.

"Thank you. For not saying anything. You should go. Everyone is staring."

"I'll go. But Casey," I wait until she meets my eyes. "I won't be forgetting about that night anytime soon. And neither will you."

❧

"I'm not sure about this new slogan." I rub my hands roughly over my face, trying not to show my frustration. "*Living the Lavin Life.* It sounds like a rip-off of a cheesy pop song."

This meeting is important, I know it is, but how am I supposed to concentrate when Clumsy Girl is sitting right down the hall from this room? *Cassandra*, I remind myself. No wonder we couldn't find her. It's a beautiful name for a beautiful woman.

A beautiful woman who wants nothing to do with me.

James holds up a hand. "Wait until you see the presentation. The campaign we've generated is youthful and high energy. Along with your name change from Lavin Fashions to Lavin Couture, it's exactly what you need for a launch into the American market."

"I hope so."

I've already seen presentations for two alternate slogans and they were no closer to capturing the essence of what we're about than the current one. As much as I like the Mirage Agency, if they can't deliver what we need then we'll have to go elsewhere. Firing our marketing team won't be fun but I haven't reached this point in my career by being soft.

I do what has to be done, even when it isn't easy.

There were so many who thought the pampered son of an aristocratic family didn't have the fortitude to run a successful business. Some are still waiting for me to fail. If I have my way, they're in for a long wait. I've waited my entire career to launch an international campaign. I won't see it derailed for any reason. Not even friendships.

Another good reason I need to pull my head out of my dick and focus.

Jason glances over me. "We're excited to see what you've come up with and ready to nail this down. Because if we don't, all of the advertising we've arranged will incur a rush fee." He grimaces as he says it. Probably because all these delays are messing with his budget.

My friend has been accused more than once of having a

calculator for a brain and a cash register for a heart. Success is his lifeblood. It's one of the things we have in common.

After a short presentation, I have to admit that the campaign is lively and fun. The team must have been anticipating that I'd object to the slogan because they've prepared a few alternates. I'm still not completely sold but it's better. Much better.

"There's a few things I'd like to change but overall ... I like it."

The entire room seems to breathe a collective sigh of relief at my words.

"Glad to hear that," Milo replies. "Now that we have a concept, we can start designing some of the ads. We're excited to get started."

Everyone stands and after shaking hands with the entire team, we're finally leaving the conference room. Just then Casey walks past the hallway carrying a cup of coffee. Jason blinks and then narrows his eyes.

Fuck. He hasn't recognized her yet and I'm not entirely sure I want him to. I step forward blocking his view. Considering how much turmoil my search for her caused around the office, I doubt he'll be thrilled to discover she's here.

"Your assistant informed us that you'll be leaving town soon," Mya says. "That's a shame. I was hoping this year you'd finally be able to attend the Preview Gala."

I stop abruptly when we reach the front of the office. The

reception area is empty. Which is odd because I just saw Casey heading this way. Maybe I can hang around for a while and wait for her to come back? I don't want to miss the chance to say goodbye and see her cheeks redden again.

Then I think of all the things I need to do this evening. There's no time for me to hang out waiting for a woman who doesn't even want to see me. I have a plane to catch and then meetings all week.

James rubs his hands together. "The Preview Gala is always a good time. The employees get a real kick out of it. It's more fun than the standard company meeting."

After a long ass day, I'm suddenly smiling. Casey may not want to talk to me but she can't exactly ignore me if we're at the same function. A function that I've been invited to.

"A company meeting? Do all of the employees usually show up?"

If James is surprised by my sudden interest, he doesn't show it. "Yes, it's mandatory for employees. Even if it wasn't, I'm sure they'd come anyway. We put on quite a party."

"Perhaps we'll stay in town." I shake hands again with James and then with Milo and Mya, promising to get in touch about the next phase in our campaign planning. My eyes follow as they walk back to their offices, looking to see if anyone emerges from the hallway.

Once we're alone, Jason leans over. "Okay, what's going

on with you? Now you want to stay in town? You hate it here."

I hold my cell phone up, trying to get a better signal. "Nothing is wrong with me. I just find myself in the mood for a party."

9

Casey

I WATCH FROM AROUND THE CORNER AS THE MAN formerly known as Andrew walks down the hall with an entourage of people including all of my bosses. Watching James, Mya and Milo shake hands with him is the perfect reminder of how incredibly screwed I am.

How am I going to explain any of this? I just started to feel comfortable here, like I know what I'm doing and am really contributing to the company.

Now all of my hard work is about to unravel and all it will take is a few words from the man I last saw naked and snoring.

The man who is currently standing in the entryway of the office looking like he doesn't have a care in the world. He's wearing a tailored, gray pinstriped suit that shows off a body that I know from experience is muscular and toned. Even the way his black hair curls over his collar is sexy.

The man is literally a walking wet dream.

He is also arrogant as hell. What was that parting shot? *I won't be forgetting about that night anytime soon. And neither will you.* Ugh, he is insufferable! How does he know that I haven't already forgotten about it? For all he knows, maybe I have one-night stands all the time and our night together was just a typical Monday night.

He pulls his cell phone from the inner pocket of his suit jacket, holding it up as if trying to get better reception. The move makes his jacket ride up. All the blood leaves my brain as he turns, giving me an award-winning view of his ass.

Nothing typical about that.

I gulp and look away for a moment. What if he turns around and catches me staring? But like a magnet, my eyes are drawn back again and again.

God, that man can wear a suit.

I lick my lips as my eyes roam over his lean arms and broad shoulders. The same arms I remember holding me down as his body powered over mine. The shoulders I hooked my legs over as he made me come again and again, like it was his mission. How many times have I woken in the early hours of the morning, damp with sweat, my breasts tight and aching after dreaming about him?

This is mental torture, remembering that night when I know it can never happen again.

I breathe a sigh of relief when Andre and the rest of his team finally get on the elevator. Once the doors close, I walk back to the reception desk. Hopefully no one noticed I left it unattended for so long.

"Hey, where did you disappear to?" Anya leans over the desk to grab her bag of potato chips. "Bingo! I knew I forgot something earlier."

"Nowhere. I was just ... uh ... getting coffee." I hold up the coffee cup I retrieved from the break room. Then I cover it with my hand before she notices that it's empty.

Anya puts a potato chip in her mouth with a loud crunch. "You're being weird."

"I'm not being weird! I'm just totally embarrassed that I crashed and burned in front of everyone earlier."

"It wasn't that bad." Anya smiles sympathetically at my skeptical look. "*Really*, it wasn't. And at least the client was nice about it. I haven't seen him be that nice in ages."

I focus on my computer screen, my fingers hitting the keyboard with way more force than necessary.

She stuffs another potato chip in her mouth. "You know,

it's funny that he should show up right after we were talking about having a fling."

My hands freeze, hovering over the keyboard. "What do you mean?"

"Well, he's exactly the kind of guy that's perfect for a casual thing. You have to pick someone who won't expect any messy romance or complications. Someone sophisticated."

I let out an exasperated breath. "I think he might be a little out of my league, Anya."

She snorts. "Well, yeah but that might be exactly why it works. He's so used to being harassed by the media when he dates actresses and Instagram models that he might actually enjoy the chance to have a fling with someone under the radar."

It's a real struggle to keep my face still. Anya has no idea just how close to the truth she is. Clearly *Andrew*, hah, was out trolling for some casual sex with someone who wouldn't recognize him the night we hooked up.

My heart sinks a little at the thought. Even though I sneaked out that night, I regretted it after that. We had a lot of fun just talking even before we left the bar. He'd seemed like a nice guy and I don't meet too many of those anymore.

Now I don't even have a good memory associated with the last time I got laid, just the bitter knowledge that Mr. Lavin was clearly slumming it when he was with me.

"Did I offend you just now? I didn't mean anything when

I said he was out of your league. He's out of *everyone's* league. Men like that are orbiting in their own galaxy. Okay, I'm shutting up now."

I laugh. "I'm not offended. But I don't have time for flings, casual or otherwise. This is the best job I've ever had and I'm trying not to screw it up. I don't have time for gossip."

Anya doesn't look convinced. "If you're going to be working with the marketing team on this, you need to make time for gossip. You need to know everything there is to know about Mr. Lavin."

Unfortunately she's right. The little bit of reading I managed to do last night before I fell asleep wasn't nearly enough. But I read enough to know this account is a big deal.

Andre Lavin is a big deal.

He's also a client.

Now I just need to convince my brain to think of him that way instead of as the best sex I'll never get to have again.

Even though I try to play it cool, I'm off my game for the rest of the day. Anya's advice is running through my head as I transfer calls and then spend some time with Mya going over the new Lavin campaign.

Ironically, the stuff she shows me is centered around Mr. Lavin's Instagram account. I've never been a big social media person so scrolling through his feed is both fascinating and humiliating all at once. I have to stop when I get to pictures of him on a yacht with a famous Hollywood actress.

Our lives couldn't be any further apart. Maybe this is the reminder I need. By the time I get home, I feel like I've just worked the longest day ever.

"Finally! You're home. Get in here."

I squeak as the door handle is snatched from my hand. Ariana grabs my arm and yanks me inside the apartment.

"What is going on?"

Ariana crosses her arms. "Mya just told me about this party tomorrow night. So I took the liberty of checking out your closet. Which is kind of boring by the way. Who doesn't have a porn stash or even a vibrator buried in the back?"

I drop my bag on the floor. "Sorry to disappoint you. I'll make sure to get something scandalous to amuse you the next time you're snooping."

My point is clearly lost on Ari who just claps her hands. "Do that. But anyway, my point is that you're going to this party, which Mya says is a big deal, but I don't see any party clothes in your closet."

"I have a black dress."

Ari grabs something from the couch. "Not this black dress, I hope?"

"What's wrong with that dress?"

She looks stricken. "There's no neckline. And it looks like

it covers your ankles. I know I've been kind of a crap room-mate but there is no way I can let you go out like this. We're going shopping. I already texted Mya."

It feels like I blink and I'm in a dressing room stall stripped down to my underwear. Mya and Ariana are outside arguing over whether or not I need stilettos. Clothes are strewn around the large space helter-skelter as if they were caught in a hurricane. Well, in a way they were.

Hurricane Ariana.

The woman is easily a category five when it comes to her powers of persuasion.

"I'm not sure how I got here. I think I just blacked out."

Anya snickers behind me. "Famous last words."

"Thanks for coming." I'd texted Anya to meet us at the store once I realized that Ariana was serious.

Since it seemed I wasn't going to be allowed to leave the apartment tomorrow night unless I had a dress that didn't look like a sack, I figured I could use Anya's expertise. She always looks amazing.

"Are you kidding? I'll take any excuse to go shopping. Here, try this one on." She hands over another dress, this one a deep amethyst color. It's the kind of thing I'd never pick out for myself but I've stopped inserting my opinions over the last hour. It's pretty clear my taste isn't working out so well.

The dress is tight so it takes a lot of work to get into it but once it's on, it fits like a glove. When I turn to look at myself in the mirror, words get stuck in my throat.

All I can come up with is, "Wow."

"You are gorgeous." Anya claps her hands and then takes a bow. She blows imaginary kisses to herself in the full-length mirror. "Yes, I know I'm brilliant. She's my greatest creation."

"I can't believe that's *me*."

I peer at the image in the mirror. Usually I avoid anything fitted because it makes me feel like every extra pound is magnified. But this dress makes those pounds look like they're all in the right places. The fabric clings and flows around my hips, making me look like I have a perfect hourglass figure. I look seductive. Confident. All the things I've always hoped to be.

"Did you find one?" Ariana's voice seems startlingly close to the dressing room door.

I hear Mya's voice next. "Move back, you weirdo. She doesn't need you eyeing her through the crack in the door like a stalker!"

I unlatch the dressing room door so they can come in.

"Damn, you look fierce." Ariana nods approvingly.

The mirror reflects four women, completely diverse in appearance but all beautiful. Normally, I'm completely content to fly under the radar but it feels good to be seen. There's no doubt in my mind that even *I* can command attention in a getup like this.

"This is a bold dress. Exactly what I need if I'm going to network with clients and make myself visible." I wish Anya and I were alone so I could ask her this next question but maybe it's fate that Mya is here, too. After all, she'd know the answer better than anyone.

"So, do most of our current clients attend? If I have to deal with the client from hell again tomorrow night, let me know now."

Mya scoffs. "Mr. Lavin? No, he never attends any of our events. To be fair, I don't blame him. That's a long way to travel just for a party."

I glance over at Anya in confusion. "A long way to travel? What do you mean?"

Mya shrugs. "It's got to be a nine hour flight, at least. Milan to DC."

"Milan?"

My confusion must be apparent because Mya stops fidgeting with her outfit in the mirror. "Yes. Mr. Lavin is Italian. Didn't I mention that? He lives in Milan."

It takes a lot of work to keep my face blank. "No, I don't think you told me that."

Anya shrugs. "It's a good thing, right? You probably won't see him for another six months, at least."

"Right. A good thing."

When I look up, Ariana is watching me in the mirror. I force a smile.

"Okay, this dress is the one. Now I just have to figure out what I'm doing with my hair."

As I take off the dress and change back into my own clothes, I remind myself that I have no reason to be sad.

No reason at all.

Casey

I FIDGET SLIGHTLY, MY FINGERS CLENCHING AROUND MY empty champagne glass as I stare up at the massive aircraft suspended in the air above my head.

The Preview Gala is being held in the National Air and Space Center, an unusual venue but absolutely stunning. Waiters in black tie scurry back and forth hefting trays of champagne, and a small ensemble band plays soft jazz in one corner. A woman glides by wearing a necklace with emeralds as large as quarters.

Not exactly my typical Saturday night.

I stand up straighter, suddenly appreciative of all the

times my mother corrected my posture and insisted I wear heels to church. We never had much money but my mother was determined to raise me the "proper" way, as a true Southern lady. I hated my mother's old-fashioned ideas growing up but am extremely thankful for them now. The other women in the room look like the type to wear lace and pearls even when they're sleeping.

I'm definitely not in Gracewell anymore.

I peer at the sign on the wall to read more about the exhibit. It's a Boeing 314. I don't know what that means but at least reading the information gives me something to do.

A passing waiter offers another flute of champagne and I take it, grateful to have something to do with my hands. I raise the glass and take a healthy gulp. Everyone else is engrossed in their conversations and no one seems to notice me, which is probably a good thing. Someone passing on my left bumps into my elbow and champagne sloshes over my hand.

"Oh hi, Casey. I didn't see you." Milo Hamilton holds my arm in a steady grip and flashes a toothy grin. "I'm usually not so clumsy."

It's impossible not to smile back at him. "No problem. Where's Mya?" A waiter appears like magic, taking my glass and handing over several napkins to mop up the spill.

"Mya hasn't arrived yet. She's coming straight from an offsite meeting with a client. Until then, I'm forced to socialize on my own." Right then the music changes to something up-tempo.

Milo holds out a hand and I take it automatically. "Let's dance."

When he moves toward the center of the floor where several couples are already dancing, that's when I start to have second thoughts.

"I'll try not to step on your feet," I joke.

He takes me through the moves of the dance, leading with gentle nudges left and right. He spins me and my mouth drops open in surprise when I don't stumble but execute a perfect turn.

"Wow. I actually did it! You make this seem so easy."

Milo winks. "I figured I should go easy on you. I appreciate you taking pity on me so I didn't have to stand by myself."

I laugh when he makes a pleading face. He's being very kind. Because I can see from the jealous looks coming from the women around us that he would have no shortage of companions if he chose to mingle. It's way more likely that he's taking pity on me.

"I'm more than happy to hang out with you. I was almost on the verge of leaving and going home."

Milo regards me thoughtfully. "I don't think you want to do that. Not until you put your admirer out of his misery."

"Admirer?" Automatically my head swivels around the room. "What are you talking about?"

Milo looks behind me pointedly. "You'll see."

I turn slowly and scan the room. People move out of the way as someone walks through. My ears start buzzing and the hair on the back of my neck stands up.

Somehow I just *know*.

Andre finally appears in the center of the crowd and comes to stand next to us. His eyes never leave mine but his words are for Milo.

"This doesn't seem fair, Mr. Hamilton. You can't keep all the beautiful women to yourself."

Milo throws his head back and laughs. He's such a handsome man with his wavy brown hair and blue eyes. But his laugh doesn't make my heart race. His touch doesn't make me lose my breath. Only one man has that effect on me and he's standing to my side, observing us with a mixture of suspicion and hostility.

"All I'm going to say, Mr. Lavin, is now we're even." Milo seems to enjoy Andre's discomfort.

I glance between the two men. "Even? What does that mean?"

Andre growls something in Italian which causes Milo to grin even harder. I cross my arms as the two continue to stare at each other.

"Hello? Will someone please tell me what's going on here?"

Milo shakes his head. "I'll leave that for Mr. Lavin to explain. I'm getting out of the line of fire." He turns and joins a group nearby.

I turn back to see Andre watching me with an intense gaze.

"Mr. Hamilton is just paying me back for a little misunderstanding that occurred while he was wooing Ms. Taylor. I'm starting to understand his position."

"Oh, you were dating Mya?" I can only hope the tremor in my voice isn't as obvious to him as it is to me.

"No. He just thought I was. That was bad enough, believe me." His eyes fix on my face. "So it'll just be the two of us. Disappointed?"

I place a hand self-consciously over my exposed cleavage. The movement draws his attention there and I watch as his pupils widen before he rips his gaze back to my face.

"Of course not. I'm always happy to talk to you, Mr. Lavin."

He grimaces. "Don't call me that. Please." The last word is less of a command and more of a plea. "Call me Andre. We're not in the office. There's no need to be formal."

I can only stare at him for a long moment. He's behaving so strangely. I have a hard time believing it really matters to him one way or the other what I call him. Especially since he didn't seem too concerned with that when we met. I let out a soft huff. I was calling him by the wrong name all night and he didn't say anything.

"Okay. Andre." Just saying his name brings a rush of heat to my cheeks. My heartbeat stutters and then begins to beat double time. "Why didn't you care this much about what I called you when we met? I was calling you Andrew all night."

"I didn't realize until it was too late. It was so loud in there and it sounds so close. I guess it doesn't matter."

But I want to tell him that it *did* matter. That everything we talked about that night has stayed with me. That for the past two months, I've wondered about the hot guy who sold men's clothes and whether he ever got the chance to do something more. Something noble.

Too bad it was all a lie.

He has all the power now. With one word to Mya or James, he can have me not only removed from the account but probably fired. According to everything I've heard, he's not a client they can afford to piss off. So I'll stand here and make polite conversation.

But I'll never again trust a word he says.

Andre

THERE ARE TIMES WHEN I QUESTION MY BELIEF IN A higher power. Too many bad people prosper while good ones suffer. But tonight, I found my belief in the principle of karma reaffirmed.

Because watching Milo Hamilton dance with Casey felt like it could only be a karmic punishment.

I glance over at her. Now that I've gotten her to myself, I should feel better but somehow having her alone still doesn't calm this irrational jealousy I feel. Maybe because I'm still seeing Milo's hands all over her bare back. Where the hell did she get that dress? Clumsy Girl wears jeans and T-shirts not satin that hugs every curve and displays an alarming amount of glowing skin.

Or is that sweat? Is she sweating because it's hot in here or because she liked dancing with Milo? Just the thought makes me crazy.

Luckily someone stops by to say hello, saving me from asking her about her dress, her sweat, or anything else that might earn me a glass of champagne to the face. The man shaking my hand vigorously is the CEO of a Fortune 500 company but I can't remember his name. My mind is a complete blank.

Well, not a blank. My mind is occupied completely with the memory of how Casey looks sweaty and wearing nothing at all.

The woman in question has drawn the CEO's attention. He eyes her appreciatively and suddenly I couldn't care any less what his name is. Casey is inching to the left slowly, like she's hoping I won't notice her moving away. Time to end this conversation. I say a pointed goodbye and then turn to Casey.

"Have you had anything to eat? Let me at least get you a drink." I look around desperately for the food.

"Oh no, you don't need to."

Maybe she doesn't need one, but I do. I grab two glasses from the tray of a passing waiter.

"So you've been at the Mirage Agency this entire time." I shake my head at the irony. "And to think, I kept blowing off those meetings. If I'd known, I would have been at the agency every day."

"Why?" She takes a small sip of her champagne, avoiding my eyes.

"What do you mean, why?"

"Why would you have come to the agency if you'd known that I was there?"

I scowl. "Because you ditched me!"

She laughs and even though it's at my expense, I'm happy to see it. At least she's talking to me now. And no longer smiling at other men.

"Don't expect me to believe that you really care about that. I'm sure you've done the same many times. Besides, if I hadn't left when I did, you would have just made up an excuse to get rid of me in the morning anyway."

"No. I wouldn't have done that. I was planning on sharing breakfast with you. Taking you home. Asking for your number."

She looks skeptical and this probably isn't the best place to discuss it anyway. Her concerns about being treated differently in a professional setting are valid. I know how people think and how the gossip mill runs. The last thing she needs is one of her coworkers overhearing this conversation.

"Come. Let's get away from the crowd. I need some air." I motion for her to follow me up the stairs to the second level.

There's a small table at the top of the stairs where we place our glasses.

Casey wanders over to the railing overlooking the floor below. "I thought you weren't coming tonight. Aren't you busy?"

"Of course. But I am learning to make time for what's important to me." I hold her gaze, wanting her to see and know the truth in my words. "Life is for living, right?"

This side of the building is in shadow, with only some muted illumination reflecting up from the main floor. From this vantage point, we can observe all of the couples mingling and dancing below. Casey shivers and I immediately slip out of my jacket and hang it on her shoulders.

"Thank you." She glances up at me, uncertainly. "You didn't have to do that."

"I wanted to."

She's about to say something else when the sound of clanking footsteps has us both turning. A woman, obviously inebriated, is coming up the stairs. Once she reaches the top, she stares at us before giggling. "*Whaaaaat?* Andre Lavin is here? Can I get a picture?"

Internally, I curse her timing. While I'm always happy to take pictures with fans, Casey looked like she was about to say something. Now she's retreated back into herself, her eyes shuttered.

It's going to be a real challenge to get her to open up

again. Especially when evidence of how different we are keeps getting thrown in her face.

"Of course," I reply, moving to stand next to the young woman.

The sound of her camera's shutter echoes in the space around us as she takes selfie after selfie, making weird faces in some and duck lips in others.

Finally she's done. "Oh my god, this is awesome!" She grabs me in a sudden hug and instantly I'm back on that red carpet watching a knife coming through the air.

I can't breathe.

By the time I've gained control of myself again, the young woman is gone. I take a shuddery breath. Panic attacks came fast and furious in the month after the incident but I thought I'd conquered those. But I've learned a hard lesson tonight. Anxiety can return at any time and in any situation.

"That happens a lot, huh?"

My heart starts pounding fast again. What does she mean? Did Casey notice my reaction? Then I realize she's talking about the woman taking my picture.

Slowly, I move back to the railing. "The fans have made me who I am."

Her eyes look down at the railing. Then I notice what has caught her attention. My hands are shaking. My fingers tighten around the balcony rail.

"Are you okay?" she asks quietly.

"Fine. Just tired." The look on her face tells me that she doesn't believe me. But I'm not ready to talk about what just happened or about what happened on the red carpet a few months before we met. So I give her the same explanation I usually give Philippe when he notices I'm not myself.

"I think I'm experiencing burnout. I used to find inspiration in the people around me, the energy of each city I visited, the sights, the sounds. But for a long time nothing has inspired me. Everything looks the same. No mystery. No excitement."

"No mystery or excitement, huh? I didn't realize I was that boring."

Fantastic. Now she thinks I'm insulting her company. "Sorry. That came out wrong. It's just this whole routine is so ... routine."

We both laugh. I look out over the venue, noting the tasteful decorations and elegantly dressed people. My heart rate slows and the tightness in my chest eases. Observing the activity below is helping to calm me down. Then Casey's arm brushes against mine and I realize that it's not the room that's soothing me.

It's her.

"I can't imagine considering champagne and five-star hotels as routine," Casey comments. "I suppose you come to a lot of parties like this. Poor baby, your life is so difficult."

Shock has me standing up straight before a smile tugs at the corners of my lips. "I sound like a spoiled brat, huh?"

"Maybe a little. But I really think you have it all wrong. People may seem predictable sometimes but they're never boring. People are complicated and fascinating."

She gestures to the level below us. A couple is dancing off to the side in a darkened corner, oblivious to everything around them. "This is a perfect example. Tell me what you see."

I squint down at the couple. "I see a couple dancing. I see this at these parties quite often. People get bored and wander off. Growing up, my brother and I were forced to attend many social events. My mother is very concerned with appearances, you see."

My memories of those parties would shock my sweet Clumsy Girl right down to her toes.

"If she only knew how many of her prim-and-proper friends we caught in compromising situations over the years, she probably wouldn't have been so insistent we attend those parties."

She nods toward the couple again. "You say they're a couple but how do you know? Just because they're dancing together?"

I lean close. "No, I assume because of the way he has his hand on her ass."

She peers over the railing again. The man has one hand firmly on the woman's bottom while the other rubs slow circles on the skin exposed by the plunging back drape of her gown. The woman stands on tiptoe to press her mouth to her lover's.

They obviously don't care that anyone can see them and I wouldn't either. If you find someone who makes you feel that way, you shouldn't care about anything but being together.

"That doesn't mean they're a couple," Casey continues, even though her face is now bright red. "Look at how they touch each other. They're so desperate. So urgent. Perhaps they're forbidden lovers. Maybe they haven't seen each other in a long time and this is their only chance to be together."

"That's very romantic."

She smiles. "But you don't agree."

"It's more likely that they're just another bored married couple who got tired of socializing. But I like your version better."

We turn to face each other and she stumbles slightly and grabs onto me to avoid falling. Her cleavage is jammed against my chest and I'm afraid to breathe because I don't want to do anything to make her move out of my arms.

"I keep having to apologize to you. Maybe that's a hint," Casey stammers.

"Haven't I already told you there's nothing to apologize for? Especially not for anything that puts you in my arms." I lower my head and brush my lips against hers. And just like every other time we've touched, it's like being engulfed in flame.

She whimpers softly and her mouth relaxes under mine. I raise one hand and tentatively touch her face. Her fingers wrap around my wrist, holding me there as her little tongue sneaks out to flick over my lips.

"Casey, sweet girl. Every time I touch you, I lose control."

Suddenly we're not in a public place where anyone could walk up on us at any moment. We're transported back to that hotel room where we were free to touch, taste, tease and tempt each other all night. Where we weren't client and employee but just two people who didn't want to be lonely for the night. Who wanted to be seen.

Casey stands on tiptoe and that changes everything. Our bodies are perfectly aligned, her breasts brushing against my chest and her hips the perfect cradle for the hard length I know she can feel pressing against her stomach. It'll be just as good this time, I can already tell. None of the fire and passion has diminished over the past few months. If anything it's only gotten stronger.

"Casey, we need to go back inside. We have to at least say goodbye to the others before we leave."

"Leave?" Her eyes fly open and dart around as if seeing things for the first time. "Oh no, we can't leave." She pushes away so quickly I'm startled into letting her go.

"What is the matter, sweetheart?" I watch, bewildered, as

Casey adjusts the straps of her dress on her shoulders and runs a hand over her mouth. I reach out to pull her back into my arms but she twists away, shaking her head furiously.

"Why are you really here tonight?" Casey whispers, her voice tortured. "Mya told me that you never come to these parties. That you live in Milan."

Ah, no wonder she's been keeping her distance.

"For you. I had to see you again. And I know that you wanted to see me again, too."

"Of course. You are so arrogant! I bet you just can't imagine any woman not wanting to ride your roller coaster for a second time, huh?"

I don't bother to suppress a dirty smile. "If I recall correctly, it was three times before we fell asleep and then you woke me with your lips all over—"

Her hands flies up to cover my mouth. "Okay, I don't need an instant replay."

"You do. And so do I. Can you really pretend that night meant nothing to you? That you want to go on with your life without experiencing it again?"

I can see the turmoil playing out all over her face. She wants this but she's scared. And I wish I could calm those fears but I just don't know how.

"Yes, that's exactly what I want," Casey finally says, taking a step back and putting her hand up to stop me from coming closer. "And since I'm sure you'll be back in Milan by tomorrow anyway, it's for the best. Good night, Andre."

A few months ago, I would have pushed for more, tried to explain that chemistry like ours cannot be denied. But I've learned you have to fight fire with a flame thrower and that timing is everything.

"Good night, Casey."

She races to the steps and clatters down so quickly I'm worried she might fall. She looks back only once, her eyes huge. Something like regret flashes across her face before she turns and continues down to the first floor.

"What the hell just happened?" I rake my hands through my hair. Up until a few minutes ago, she was right there with me. I can still taste her and feel her soft curves torturing me. But considering I just mauled her in a semipublic place where any of her coworkers could have walked by, I'm lucky she didn't slap me.

I deserve it.

I let out a long, slow breath. I pushed her too hard and scared her off. I just keep getting it wrong.

Footsteps clang on the staircase behind me and I whip around, hoping maybe Casey came back. Milo Hamilton stands there smirking.

He glances down at my obviously aroused state. "Things not going so well?"

"Apparently not." His knowing laugh follows me as I push past and walk down the stairs to the main level.

She thinks this is the end of it and that we've cleared the air. She's expecting to show up to work on Monday and have her life continue exactly as it did before, our little tryst a thing of the past.

It's almost enough to make me feel guilty for what I'm planning.

Almost.

Casey

I STRUGGLE UP THE STEPS TO MY APARTMENT BUILDING, my heels getting caught in the grooves of the concrete staircase. After my mad dash from the balcony I ran directly into Anya, who took one look at my wild eyes, tousled hair and swollen lips and offered to drive me home. Anya was tactful enough not to ask me what I'd been doing. I can only hope no one else noticed my hasty departure.

Or saw me getting up close and *very* personal with a client.

I unlock the door and toss my keys on the entry table

where they land with a clatter next to the mail. My shoes come off next and then at last, my bra.

Now that feels better.

When I open my eyes, Ariana is standing in the kitchen. "Rough night?"

I shrug and swipe a hand over my hair self-consciously. Even though I looked fine when I checked my reflection in the car, I just *feel* disheveled. Like everyone else can tell I've been making out with someone I shouldn't be.

"How was your first big company event? Fun? Boring?" Ariana leans down to inspect the contents of the refrigerator.

"It was nice. Lots of food and free champagne."

Ariana stands suddenly. "Free booze? Mya didn't tell me that! Damn, I should have gone."

"Yeah, I probably had a little too much."

All of a sudden I just want to tell someone. Keeping this secret is going to be really hard and I can't tell Anya or anyone else I work with. I just need one person I can vent to who will understand and can give me some advice.

Ariana is out there but she also seems like she knows a lot about dating and all the bullshit that comes with that. I need someone to tell me what I'm supposed to do in this situation because I have no idea.

"Can you keep a secret?"

She folds her hands over her mouth. "Does the secret

have anything to do with why you came home from a company party with just-fucked hair?"

"Damn it!" I rush over to the mirror next to the entryway and then swipe at the lock of hair that's falling waywardly over my ear. "That means I left the event looking like this!"

Ariana plops down on the couch. "It could have been from too much dancing or maybe you fell because you drank too much. As long as no one saw you do anything, it didn't happen."

I turn slowly. "That's the part I'm not sure about."

"Tell me. You know you want to."

With a sigh, I drop down onto the couch next to her, the purple satin of my dress bunching beneath me. "First, you have to promise not to tell anyone. What's revealed on this couch has to stay on the couch. No one, Ariana. Not even Mya. *Especially* not Mya."

"Wait, why especially not Mya? Oh no, you don't mean that Milo ... "

"No, no, no. Definitely not." I'm really screwing this up. Now I've got her questioning whether her best friend's husband is a scumbag. "Not him. But someone else that Mya knows. Do you know who Andre Lavin is? He's one of the agency's clients."

Her mouth drops open. "Wait, the hot, Italian designer guy? I remember when Mya was trying to land that account. It was a big deal."

"Yes! It's a big, huge deal. And maybe no one saw what happened but if they did, I'm going to get fired. I don't want to be fired, Ari. I can't go back to being broke and living in that scary motel!" I'm not even sure I can make sense of my ramblings at this point but hopefully Ariana gets the point.

"Okay, let's just calm down," Ariana says in the kind of delicate voice you use when you're trying to keep a rabid animal from attacking.

Not that it's far off the mark. The enormity of how messed up this all is has finally hit me and I am panicking.

"I can't calm down. The people at work are just getting to know me and I'm starting to make friends. I don't want to start over somewhere else."

"That's not going to happen. It was just ... " She looks at me expectantly.

"A kiss. He kissed me on the balcony upstairs. Then I ran off."

"Okay, a kiss is not that bad." She lets out a sudden laugh. "Damn, you had me worried for a second. I thought you were going to say you boned in a closet or something."

I let out a soft whine before I can stop it.

She points at me. "You didn't bone in a closet after the kiss, did you?"

"No, we didn't ... do that. At least, not tonight."

Ariana just blinks. "This doesn't happen often but I have no idea what to say. And I thought you were boring at first."

I snort out a laugh. "Well, I'm not sure having a one-night stand with a guy and then finding out who he is two months later is what I want to be known for."

"And you won't be. It happened and now it's over. Was he a jerk to you?" She looks enraged on my behalf.

"No. He was ... I'm not sure what he was. He's so ... so ... I don't know. The man thinks he's such a gift to women. Like he was so shocked that I didn't want to pick up where we left off two months ago, as if the fact that he lied about who he is doesn't even matter. Ugh, he makes me so mad! But then he can be so sweet sometimes."

"*Uh-oh.*"

I break off in the middle of my tirade to find Ariana watching me with horror. "What?"

"You like him," she accuses.

"*No, I don't.* He's a jerk a lot of the time and also he thinks he's such hot stuff hanging out with actresses on his yacht. And he doesn't even live here. But really, who needs a boat that big, huh? Only guys who are compensating for something get boats that big."

She raises an eyebrow. "Well, is he compensating for something?"

I scowl. "Unfortunately, no. Damn it, this is not how things are supposed to be. He was supposed to be a random guy I'd never see again, not a client. That was the whole point of a one-night stand, to keep me from having to deal with this stuff. What are people going to say when they find out?"

Ariana claps her hands. "Casey, you are a hot little number. Own it. Work it. Don't let anybody make you feel ashamed. You were both consenting adults. Do you think he's going to rat you out to your boss?"

Instinctively, I shake my head. "No, I don't think he would do that. Plus, he'll be in Europe anyway. Mya said that's where he usually is."

"Well, there you go. It's over. It's done. It's nobody else's business. You're going to go back to work on Monday, hold your head high and be the best damn receptionist ever."

Her pep talk is actually working. It'll be embarrassing if anyone saw us, sure. But she's totally right. We're adults. It's not like anyone was forced into doing something they didn't want to do. If James brings it up, I won't lie. But really, as long as Andre doesn't complain, why would James even care? I can't be the first person who has had too much to drink at a company party and done something they shouldn't have.

"You're right. It's nobody's damn business."

Ariana fist pumps the air. "That's the spirit. Now I'm going to pick out some power outfits for you to borrow. Trust me, it'll make you feel more confident if you look like a boss bitch."

I walk back to my room and carefully wiggle out of my dress. It was nice to feel like a princess for a little while but being glamorous is hard work. It's so much easier to just curl up in my favorite pajamas and read a good book. A few minutes later Ari comes in with an armful of clothes.

"These should fit and don't worry, they're all office appropriate. Tomorrow is a new day. A new beginning!" She grins. "Maybe I should consider a career as a motivational speaker. I'm pretty good at this crap."

She turns to go but then stops. "You said you won't be seeing him anytime soon, right?"

I shake my head. "I doubt it. From what I've heard he rarely comes in to the office and he lives in Italy anyway."

"Oh, well that's lucky."

"Yeah it is. It would have been really awkward if I had to see him every day."

"For sure. Also you don't have to worry about any revenge ego."

I'm not sure if this is Ariana-speak or if that's an actual thing that I should be aware of. I've heard of revenge porn which is bad enough. The thought that anyone could do that to someone they were once intimate with makes me sick to my stomach.

"Am I supposed to know what that means?"

She shakes her head. "It's the kind of thing you only know about if you've ever gotten between a powerful man and his ego. Men like this are different. They're used to getting what they want, when they want it. If he was someone you had to see all the time, I would warn you to be on your toes. Because men like this always seek revenge for their wounded egos."

Now she's making me nervous. I don't think Andre would seek any kind of revenge on me just because I don't want to sleep with him again. Just the thought makes me feel uncomfortable. Because if he ever did, it would mean I am officially a terrible judge of character.

"I guess it's a good thing he's not around much then."

"Yeah. Like I said, lucky. Good night!"

She closes the door, leaving me alone with a pile of her clothes and a vague sense of unease.

The rest of the weekend I spend doing homework and laundry. Monday morning, I repeat Ariana's words while I get ready. The outfits she left for me aren't exactly my definition of office appropriate but they're still better quality than anything I own. Since the sweaters all expose quite a bit of cleavage, I decide to tie a scarf around my neck to tone it down.

On the metro ride in to work, I catch several guys checking me out. Maybe this outfit was a mistake.

"Morning!" I beam brightly at Anya as I walk through the lobby and then take my seat behind the reception desk.

"Someone is in a good mood this morning."

Okay, maybe I shouldn't be quite so peppy. I want people to see me as professional not ditzy.

"Just trying to keep a positive mindset."

Anya waves at one of the guys from the legal department who gives me a leer as he walks by. What was that look for? Am I showing too much cleavage or was he at the party Saturday night and saw me nearly sucking the lips off our biggest client?

The uncertainty is going to bug me all day. Every time someone looks at me sideways I'm going to wonder if they saw me. Meanwhile Andre is probably in Milan by now eating caviar for breakfast, or whatever it is that billionaires enjoy with their coffee.

Resolved not to think about it, I focus on answering the phone while doing some research on the computer for Mya. One of her clients is a mid-level lingerie brand so she has me compiling images of their competitor's products. I never thought I'd be looking at pictures of thongs for work, but here we are.

When I come back from lunch, I'm getting ready to go to Mya's office when Milo approaches the reception desk. Anya should be here soon to relieve me.

"Afternoon, Casey. Did you already set up conference room three?"

"There's a conference this afternoon? I don't remember seeing any appointments." I pull up the calendar for the day.

There's nothing but internal meetings which are usually held in private offices. All of the conference rooms are available. "There must be a mistake ... "

"Actually it's my fault." James walks up, hands held out in surrender. "The Lavin Group asked for a meeting this afternoon."

My heartbeat comes to a screeching halt in my chest. "The Lavin Group? Andre Lavin is coming back *today*?"

Both men peer at me strangely. James nods slowly. "At three o'clock. I sent Anya a message last night reminding her to put it on the calendar. She's usually really great at keeping up with these sorts of details."

I swallow against the sudden hard knot in the middle of my throat. "It must have slipped her mind."

My insides go hot. If James sent the message yesterday, that means Andre called him to schedule the meeting *after* the Preview Gala was over. After I told him to go back to Europe and leave me alone.

Now he's coming here and it's probably not going to mean anything good for me.

And there's no way Anya forgot about this. The little traitor is playing matchmaker without knowing she's two months too late. Now her innocent little trick to surprise me is about to blow up in ways she couldn't have imagined.

"It's no problem at all." I take a few deep breaths before

continuing. "Just let me know what you need and I'll get everything set up."

James looks stricken. "Sorry it's so last minute. Anya must have forgotten. I usually check on these things, but then I ... Well, I forgot, too."

Milo's lips twitch. "It shouldn't take long to set up the room. We just need some refreshments and an extra set of hands to distribute the marketing materials."

I carefully remove my headset. "I'm on it. I'll go see if Anya is available to help as well." It's work to keep my steps light and even as I walk away. As soon as I round the corner out of their sight, I break into a sprint.

"Whoa! Where's the fire?" Anya pokes her head out of the copy room. "Who are you running from?"

"I'm not running from anyone. I was trying to find you." I push her back into the room and close the door. Anya avoids my gaze, suddenly interested in the stacks of paper on the worktable in front of her.

"Is he here already?" At least she has the grace to look guilty.

"Who exactly are you referring to, Anya? I don't have anything on the schedule for this afternoon. I'm sure you wouldn't purposely omit telling me about an appointment that was rescheduled."

"Don't be so dramatic. I didn't tell you because I knew

you'd just worry about it all day. You're so shy and I figured you just needed a little push. I already set up the refreshments so all that's needed are the handouts for the presentation."

"I hate being caught off guard. I'm already out of my league as it is."

Anya picks up a large stack of paper and hands it to me. "Just follow my lead. It's fine. Everything is under control."

I follow her out of the copy room, internally debating whether there's enough time to pretend to be sick or suddenly remember I have a doctor's appointment. But it's already almost three o'clock so the best I can do is grit my teeth and try to get through this without any mishaps.

Anya walks down to the largest conference room and immediately crosses to the sideboard where the food has been set up. James walks up and says something that causes Anya to turn her back to him. He stands there staring at the stiff set of her shoulders for a moment before walking away.

At least Andre isn't here yet. I hug the stack of papers against my chest and let out a soft breath of relief. I still have some time to get myself together. I turn around and slam into something that feels like concrete.

"Ouch!"

I clutch frantically at the sheets of paper but it's no use. Dozens of white sheets flutter to the floor and scatter across the room. Everything goes completely still including the body I just crashed into.

The very firm, black-suited body.

"Hello again, Cassandra."

I murmur hello before I kneel and start gathering the handouts. So much for gritting my teeth and getting through this. I was hoping I could hide out in the back of the room and then just hurry out as soon as the meeting was over.

It's unnaturally quiet in the room. I look up to see that everyone is watching. To be precise, they're watching the man now kneeling on my right.

Andre Lavin is actually down on the floor collecting the papers at his feet into a neat pile. Great. I close my eyes. Not only is everyone staring, but I've got the agency's biggest client scrabbling around on the floor.

"You don't have to do that. You'll get all dirty." I take the pile of paper he's collected and tug at his arm.

"I don't mind. It was my fault after all." He stands in one swift motion. "Besides, I don't mind getting a little dirty."

A slow, suggestive grin spreads over his face and my heart trips so hard I'm afraid I'll drop everything all over again. Just to be safe, I set it all down on the conference table. Damn that man and his smile. That thing is like a loaded weapon!

Anya walks over and picks up half the handouts. Everyone else has finally turned their attention to other things but I still feel conspicuous.

Probably because Andre is still staring and not doing anything to disguise it.

"Well, well, well. I guess you don't need my help at all. It looks like he wouldn't mind if you tripped and fell against him anytime." Anya raises her eyebrows before walking to the other side of the conference table.

Andre strokes the square piece of fabric tucked into the front pocket of his suit. I've seen men wear those before but usually they're the same color as their tie. It's odd because this one seems to be some kind of weird pattern. I squint. Are those unicorns?

"*Oh sweet baby Jesus!*" I holler, horrified as I realize what that little pocket square is about.

James is just entering the room at the time of my outburst. "Are we ready to get started?"

Panicked, I look around frantically, wishing I could sink through the floor. Is he really wearing a pocket square made from my panties? As much as I wish that was impossible, the last time I saw that particular pattern was on the panties I forgot in the hotel room we shared.

Andre blinks innocently. "Feeling all right, Miss Michaels?"

I narrow my eyes. I know what he's doing wearing that stupid thing and it's not going to work. He is not going to get the best of me.

"Of course, *Mr. Lavin*. I was just ... praying. I'm very religious. Have you been told the good news about Jesus lately?"

Andre looks like he's on the verge of laughing but

manages to hold it together. "Maybe later. I must say James, your employees have been so welcoming. I've never had such good service. "

James looks back and forth between us in confusion. "Well, we're very tolerant here at Mirage of all religions and customs."

Andre takes his seat at the end of the table. But every few seconds his eyes find mine again. Did he fall and bump his head or something? It's almost like he doesn't remember what happened on Saturday night.

Until his eyes drop to my breasts and his lips curl into a small smile.

I cough and turn away, trying to get my breathing under control. The lights dim slightly, which prods me into action. I have work to do and the agency isn't paying me to stand around and ogle handsome men. Even irresistible Italian ones.

Everyone takes their seats as the presentation begins. Not for the first time, I marvel at how fluidly Milo and Mya work together. They each present a separate section of the presentation and at times finish each other's sentences when one or the other gets stuck explaining a point.

It must be wonderful to have someone who understands you that way.

I circle the table, distributing the handouts relevant to the next part of the presentation. Anya has already given them out on her side of the conference table, leaving me to hand them to Andre and the other members of his company.

There's Jason Gautier, a tall, blond man who I remember from my notes is the Chief Operating Officer and a pinch-faced woman I've never seen. She regards me icily before turning her attention back to the front.

As I approach Andre, I look for an excuse not to get too close to him. Finally, I place the handout on the table but he reaches out and takes it so our fingers brush. I snatch my hand back at the contact, determined to ignore the thrill of his touch. It's an impossible task, especially since I know what those strong, slender fingers are capable of.

Andre regards me thoughtfully before speaking to the rest of the group.

"Let's test it out."

Everyone at the table turns to face him. I back up and stand off to the side. I'm not sure what the next section of the program is about but it won't hurt for me to stay out of the way.

Milo and Mya exchange confused looks. James shifts in his seat. He opens his mouth but after a glance at Andre's determined face, he stays silent.

"I want to finalize the marketing campaign before the holidays. Our art department also needs time to make changes to our print advertising planned for Fashion Week early next year." Andre runs his hands over his hair and sighs. "We're wasting time we don't have."

"What do you mean test it out?" Mya asks. "Do you want us to set up a focus group and survey different demographics–"

Andre stands. "No time for that. This is the third slogan we've tried, so I think it's time we get a little creative. Besides, we have a member of our prime demographic group right here."

Then he turns toward me and smiles.

"I don't feel so lucky anymore," I mutter under my breath.

13

Andre

I walk over to Casey and take her by the hand. Eyes wide, she follows me to the front of the room.

"Oh my god, I should have known you were pissed about Saturday night. This is how you get your revenge, huh? Men and their egos," she hisses before smiling nervously at everyone watching.

"Stop fidgeting," I whisper.

Finally she stops moving and folds her hands in front of her nervously. I walk over to the computer running the presentation and use the mouse to navigate back to one of the campaign images previously displayed. It depicts a young man wearing a sleek, black suit. The slogan *"Livin' the Lavin Life"* is splashed across the top of the photo in red.

"When you see this advertisement, what is the first thing that pops into your mind?"

Casey looks terrified before glancing over her shoulder at me. When she sees I'm legitimately waiting for her answer, she turns back to the photo.

"Um ... I don't know. This is my first advertising job. I don't know much about this stuff."

When I notice her glancing over her shoulder again, I follow her gaze. Everyone is watching us. Mya looks nervous whereas Milo seems amused. James, on the other hand, seems furious. I'm sure he doesn't appreciate how I've taken over his meeting.

I lean a little closer to Casey. "Uh-uh, *piccolina*. Don't look at them, look at the picture. Just tell me how it makes you feel."

Casey heaves a great sigh. I wonder what she sees when she looks at this. I see a man who is thin, handsome and dark-haired, the typical look of a male fashion model. The colors are vibrant and there is a diverse group of people in the background. Still, there is something *off* about the whole thing.

And I can't articulate what it is.

When Casey sees me staring at her, waiting, she shrugs. "The ad is perfect. It's fun and energetic. There's nothing wrong with the ad."

After a few moments of silence, she follows that with, "It's just not what I would associate with you."

Behind us James lets out a soft groan. There are a few soft titters of laughter. Casey looks over her shoulder and cringes.

As for me, I throw back my head and laugh until there are tears in my eyes.

I put my arm around her shoulders, anchoring her to my side. "This is *exactly* what I've been feeling. The question is why? I am a fun guy, no?"

All motion behind us stops. I'm sure all of the Mirage employees are glaring at her but Casey squares her shoulder and looks me right in the eyes.

"Barbecues and basketball games are fun. You are *not* fun. You're too sophisticated for such a simplistic word and that's why this advertisement doesn't work. I just don't see you as a wild, crazy guy going out on the party scene."

I eye the picture again. "You're right. For example, I couldn't see myself in that room with those people."

"Exactly." Casey points at the outfit the model is wearing. "I also can't see you wearing that so casually. You're just not a casual sort of man. This needs to be more elegant, more refined. The type of party where they serve champagne instead of beer."

"Like Saturday night, hmm?" I keep my voice low so the others don't hear.

Casey narrows her eyes and whispers, "Do not tease me about that. It should have never happened."

There's a sharp, pointed sound of someone clearing a throat. She peeks over her shoulder and then bites her lip. "It's just my opinion. Like I said, I don't know anything about advertising."

I decide to put her out of her misery. "We've made good progress today. Let's reconvene in one week's time."

The room immediately erupts into sound. Milo and Mya launch into a barrage of questions. James looks like he needs an antacid.

Surprisingly, in the midst of all the chaos, James's assistant, Anya is the one who takes control. "So, we're meeting next week again? What day will you be flying in?" She grips a small yellow legal pad, hand poised to jot down the date.

My eyes cut over to Casey quickly. "I won't be flying in."

All the air in the room seems to dry up as I hold her gaze. She shakes her head slightly. "Oh no," she whispers.

"I don't plan on going back to Italy until this is resolved." With that bombshell, I lean over to Casey and whisper, "I'm picking you up after work. Meet me outside or I'm coming in to get you."

The minute hand on my watch has barely passed five o'clock when the doors to the Madison building fly open and Casey comes storming out. Her eyes roam over everyone walking past before they land on me. The look on her face can only be described as rage.

Someone is definitely not happy to see me.

"What was that up there?"

I shake my head. "Somehow I don't think you really want to have this conversation in front of your building. Come on."

She follows as I lead her down the sidewalk, her legs working double-time to keep up. "Where are we going?"

I don't respond other than to take her arm and guide her around the corner to a small café I found while waiting for her. It's a cute little French place with a green and white striped awning.

She looks around with interest. "I've seen this place before but never had time to stop."

"Well, today we are making time." I hold out a chair for her at one of the small wrought iron tables. "I'm in the mood for beignets."

"I've had those before. Anya brings them to work sometimes."

A waitress appears then, smiling flirtatiously before asking what we'd like to drink. Casey rolls her eyes as the simpering blonde writes down our order with a series of unnecessary hair flips.

Once she's gone, Casey slumps back in her chair. "I'm sure your cup of coffee will come with her phone number scrawled across the bottom."

I shrug. "And it will end up in the trash. She's not my type."

"Yeah I've seen your type. Your Instagram page is fascinating."

"It should be. I pay a whole team of people to make it that way."

She looks away. "So, you're saying that's not accurate? You don't really spend all your time lounging on yachts feeding grapes to supermodels?"

Dio, that mouth. Has fighting with a woman ever been so stimulating?

"Oh no. I only feed grapes to supermodels on special occasions."

Fed up, Casey finally meets my eyes directly. "What are we doing here?"

Before I can answer the waitress returns with a basket of steaming hot beignets and our drinks, a small cappuccino for her and an espresso for me. Once we're alone again, I take an appreciative sip of my espresso, enjoying the ability to just relax for a moment. That's what Casey does for me. With her, I feel no pressure to perform or be interesting or impressive. I can just ... exist.

Casey bangs her fists on the table suddenly. "What does

all this mean? You can't just put me on the spot in front of everyone like you did today! I can't afford to lose this job." Her voice breaks a little on the last words.

"*Cara mia*, you will not lose your job." I put my cup down and lean across the table. "I apologize. I should have explained right away. Mr. Lawson mentioned you've been assisting the designers. I already requested the agency assign you to work on my account. Welcome to the team."

She sits back, stunned. "I don't understand any of this. And just because we have this ... *attraction* ... between us, doesn't mean you should lie and say this is about work. Somehow I doubt James will let me anywhere near this campaign after what I said today."

"I will do many things but I rarely lie. An intelligent man doesn't need to. You will be working on my account. For what I'm paying this agency, they'd assign the janitor to work on the account if I asked them to."

Casey laughs. Other diners turn to stare and she claps a hand over her mouth to stifle it. "You really have gone mad. I am the *last* person you should want working on this. You saw what happened in that meeting today. James was furious. I'm lucky if I still have a job after this."

I scoot my chair closer to hers. "Casey, you are the only one who understands what I'm about. You saw those campaigns the others designed for me. They do great work but it wasn't right for *me*." I tap the tip of her nose gently.

"On their own, they seem to have no idea what appeals to me. You're the only one who gets it. You can at least tell the designers if they're on the right track."

She seems to be thinking about it. This close, I can see every emotion on her face. I'm not sure if she knows how easily she telegraphs her thoughts.

Finally, she takes a small sip of coffee. "No funny business, right? I mean, it's all professional?"

I struggle to put my most innocent expression on my face. "Of course. I'd like to think we can be friends."

"You think we can be friends with everything that's happened?"

"Why not?"

"Because, I don't know. I've seen you *naked*." She looks around hurriedly. "That's not exactly a thing friends do."

"You'd be surprised."

She rolls her eyes. "Well, I'm not looking for naked friends. So that means we're just doing this marketing campaign thing."

I nod. "That's all. Just business. Now I've asked my assistant to find some time for you to meet with our social media team so you can get familiar with our corporate culture and image. Once you get a sense of what we're about, it'll be easier for you to make recommendations to the rest of the marketing team."

"Okay. That doesn't sound so bad."

"Great. Let's go."

She gapes at me. "What, right now?" After taking a final gulp of her drink, she stands too. "I thought you meant tomorrow. Or next week."

"No time like the present. Besides, I have something I want to show you." After I throw some money down on the table, I gesture for her to walk ahead of me.

Casey starts walking but then spins around and slaps both hands on my chest. "Remember what I said. No funny business."

14

Casey

Half an hour later, I fold my hands nervously in front of me, scared to touch anything. One minute I was at the café agreeing to what seemed like a rational business proposal, and the next I'm twenty stories off the ground in a penthouse almost as big as the Mirage offices.

This is definitely funny business, I think as I look around. *The funniest of business.*

Andre disappeared immediately, telling me to make myself at home. Hah! Nothing about this is remotely like home.

I turn in a slow circle, awed by the wide expanse of space.

Everything in the place is white, black or stainless steel. A wall of windows lets in tons of natural light. It's beautiful. It's also perfectly decorated and utterly cold.

"Come. Let's get you comfortable." Andre reappears at my elbow and leads me gently to a large, white sectional sofa.

I cross my arms. "I think I'd rather stand. Why are we here? You said you wanted me to work with your social media team."

The man must think I am really naive. He told me he wanted to work on business and then brought me to his penthouse where we're completely alone. Nothing in the world is going to make me comfortable except perhaps a Valium or a bottle of vodka.

"Cassandra, relax. I won't bite you. That's not why we're here." Andre sits on the other end of the sofa, reclining casually into the large cushions. "I actually want to show you something personal."

I throw my hands up. "Seriously? Again with the innuendo."

He doubles over laughing. "That sounded bad. Although to be fair if I wanted to show you my cock I wouldn't be nervous. I already know you like that. I want to show you something work-related."

I let the remark about liking his dick slide. That's a rabbit hole I refuse to jump into. "Oh. Well, what do you want to show me here?" I look around the room. Nothing is out of place so I'm not sure what he could be referring to.

He rubs his hands together. "Actually, I'm trying to get my nerve up to bring it out. I've never shown anyone else."

I sit on the edge of the couch. Honestly, seeing him nervous has made me relax. He's so calm and in control all the time that it's a refreshing change to see him thrown off a bit. Maybe he's actually normal like the rest of us.

"I'm not exactly a fashion queen, remember? I'm not sure why my opinion matters."

His head lifts and his eyes spear mine. "It matters to me." After a moment, he stands and then disappears down a hallway across from the room we're in. He comes back a few minutes later carrying a mannequin. He sets it carefully in the middle of the floor and I come to stand next to him. The mannequin is dressed in a pair of trousers that look like a cross between cargo pants and dress pants.

Andre runs a hand over the fabric. "The material is a combination of nylon and merino wool. It's comfortable and light but durable enough for hiking. It will wick away moisture quickly and breathes well. But they look more like a pair of dress pants than the typical hiking gear."

I reach out to touch the material, careful to avoid the pins sticking out of all the seams. "Wow. So it's activewear but looks more like high fashion wear."

His eyes sparkle at the description. "This is it, exactly.

Clothes that are about more than what they look like. People have this image of who I am: cool, urbane and aloof. Lavin style has always reflected that."

"You don't think that's an accurate representation?" From what I saw on his Instagram feed, his style is very similar to what he's been wearing the past few days. Perfectly tailored suits that he wears so effortlessly they might as well be jeans.

"It's not that it's inaccurate. Just incomplete. I'm more than just that. I enjoy hiking, biking, running and swimming. That's what I want to create, clothes for men that allow them to look good while truly living."

"Sounds pretty brilliant to me."

He doesn't say anything but his lips turn up at the corners. "I assure you it's considered sacrilege in some circles."

"Well, those circles don't sound like the ones I would want to be in. Do you have anything else?"

He holds up a finger and then disappears down the hallway again. When he comes back carrying another mannequin, I have to hold in a snort of laughter. This one is wearing a coat so puffy that I can barely see his face.

"What are you laughing at?"

"You look like the Abominable Coat Man carrying that thing."

"The panels are meant for winter weather so each one is

triple-filled. It's also designed to zip completely closed so it can double as a sleeping bag."

I look closer and notice the extra zipper across the bottom. Suddenly I remember that he told me about this two months ago. The rush of warmth at the memory is unexpected. Apparently everything he told me wasn't a lie.

The thought brings me more comfort than it should. Since we're supposed to be just friends and all.

"This is what you mentioned that night. Making clothes that can help the less fortunate."

He looks shocked. "Yes. It was only a vague idea at the time but after that night, I decided to make a sample. I figured if I could come up with a design that could make use of some of the scraps from our production process, then it would help someone while also recycling at the same time."

I watch as he tugs at the panels on the coat. "What happened? If you made a sample, why aren't these coats being produced?"

"Because the Board of Directors shot it down. They didn't want Lavin fabric being used on something that was being given away. They worry about it devaluing the brand."

Shocked, I watch him continue to fiddle with the pins. I can't even begin to understand that logic. "Wait, so they'd rather throw all that extra fabric away than give it to someone who could use it?"

He nods sadly. "It's very common in the fashion industry,

actually. Many brands will destroy or burn their extra inventory just so it won't be sold at a discount. They don't want anyone they don't deem worthy using their products."

"That's disgusting."

"I agree."

I watch him messing with the panels on the coat. It hits me then that I'm probably the only person he can talk to about this. If you'd asked me just an hour ago if I thought Andre Lavin was lonely, I would have laughed. The man is rich, famous and at the top of his career. But as I watch him gaze lovingly at a puffy coat, I realize that he can be all of those things and lonely at the same time.

Maybe he feels just as trapped by his life as I do by mine sometimes.

"Well, I think it's amazing. It's a really creative design."

He dips his head slightly before murmuring, "*Grazie*. I just wish I'd fought harder at the time for the idea."

"Maybe you still can. This new marketing campaign can be an opportunity to try again. The board might see it differently if we can prove how beneficial a non-profit program will be to the company's image."

He slides his hands in his pockets. "You're good at this. And I can see how happy this job makes you."

"It does. Working with Mya has been so interesting. She's really smart and has handled so many different companies. I've learned a lot from her already."

"She designed a fantastic campaign for Lavin Bridal last year. I was impressed."

Last year. Thinking of him working closely with Mya last year makes me think about what Milo said at the Preview Gala. If they were working so closely on the campaign, is that why Milo thought they were dating? Or was it something more?

"I guess you know her pretty well then."

His enigmatic smile reveals nothing. "Are you asking as a friend?"

"Of course. I was just wondering." I lean down and grab my handbag. "I should probably go. Ariana will be wondering where I am."

"Let me drive you home. I didn't mean to keep you so late. Time got away from me."

"You don't have to do that." But I already know what he's going to say.

"I want to. What kind of friend would I be if I didn't make sure you got home safely?"

His insistence on using the word seems significant. Something tells me he's going to make me regret asking to be just friends.

It doesn't take that long to get to my apartment but I spend the entire ride wishing I didn't have to go home. But I know that if I stayed any later, it would be really difficult to stick to my side of the *just friends* bargain.

Andre is arrogant and maddening and all of those other things I complained about to Ariana. But he's also a creative genius and incredibly attuned to me. Despite all the outrageous things he says and does, I get the feeling he's just enjoying my honest reactions to him. From what I've observed, that's not something he gets to experience often.

Everyone seems to either treat him like a business or like a god. Neither of which is going to keep anyone warm at night. And even though I'm sure attempting to be his friend is probably like asking a fox to be a friend to a hen, I'm still going to attempt it.

Even if there's the chance this will go badly, I *want* to be his friend. I like him. And I like how much he seems to like me.

"You're awfully quiet over there."

The car pulls smoothly to the side of the road. There's rarely any parking in Adams Morgan at this time of night so we're double-parked. Andre's strong features are illuminated in the light from the nearby building.

"Just thinking about tonight. I was pleasantly surprised. I really didn't think you could get through an entire night without doing something inappropriate."

He grins. "You shouldn't speak so soon. You're not home yet."

"So this is where you fall off the wagon, huh? Well, go ahead then. Get it over with so I can slap you and call it a night."

His smile falls away as he leans closer, leaning on the center console of the car to get closer. My breath speeds up as I take in the scent of his aftershave. I close my eyes anticipating another scorching kiss like the one he gave me at the Preview Gala.

When his lips press firmly to my forehead, my eyes fly open to meet his. His finger trails over my cheek gently.

"You didn't ... "

"You asked me to respect your wishes and that is what I will do."

Maybe he's even more brilliant than I thought if he already has me cursing my own damn rules. Why did I have to say all that stuff about being professional? In the moment I'm finding it hard to remember all the reasons I thought getting naked again was a bad idea. And friends? What was I thinking?

The way I'm feeling toward him right now is anything but friendly.

"Since you're being so accommodating maybe I should have asked you for a few more things while I was at it. Mirage could use a new coffeemaker for the break room, for instance."

He cups my cheek gently. "I wonder sometimes how dangerous you would be if you knew your own power. Don't you know I would give you anything you asked for? Anything at all."

He growls softly when I bite my lip. "Get out of the car, Casey."

I look over at him, not surprised to see the same tortured expression on his face that I'm feeling.

"Go on, sweetheart. I need to make sure you're safely inside."

With a sigh, I push open the door. I can feel his eyes on me the entire time as I walk away.

But I don't look back.

Andre

I PUT DOWN THE SKETCH IN MY HANDS AND STAND. How long have I been at this? The clock on the wall shows it's almost lunchtime. It's amazing how time moves when you're trying to distract yourself from something.

Driving away from Casey's building last week was difficult. Every part of me wanted to follow her upstairs, see where she lives, sleep with her in her bed.

Despite how many times she's made it clear that what we shared is over, there's a certain part of my anatomy that refuses to accept it. I look down at the anatomy in question.

Every man has a unique relationship with his cock. You

have to when dealing with something that has a mind of its own. These things lead us around by the nose quite often and mine has been particularly unhappy with my decisions lately.

But then I remember the look on her face when I kissed her forehead. Surprise, yes, but also hope. Even though I don't know her whole story yet, I get the sense that men often let her down.

So no matter how angry a certain part of me has been lately, I'll continue to give her what she needs. A friend.

Plus, even with an ego like mine, I have to admit that she could have taken things further in the car if she'd wanted to. There was nothing stopping her from leaning over and kissing me like she did that night in the bar. Or unhooking her seatbelt and climbing into my lap.

But she didn't. The past few days she hasn't given me any indication that she wants to see me. Hell, she could have called if she was feeling any of the things I am.

Then it hits me. She still doesn't have my phone number.

I'm actually sitting here moping because she hasn't called me when I never gave her my number. I have to laugh. My friends would tease me until the end of time if they could see how much Casey throws me off my game.

Voices filter through my closed door, pulling me from my thoughts.

"Oh no, please don't disturb him!"

"It's no problem. Mr. Lavin made it clear that marketing is a high priority."

Who is that Kate is talking to? I check my watch. It's definitely not time for the board meeting yet. Things have been quiet around the office. Most of our employees, besides the design team we brought with us, are American so they were gone to celebrate Thanksgiving last week. Things have been pretty quiet. It would have been an excellent time to get some work done if I could actually concentrate.

The phone on my desk rings. I hit the button to activate the speaker. "Yes, Kate."

"Mr. Lavin, a Cassandra Michaels is here to see you from the Mirage Agency."

It's a wonder I don't break the button with how fast I hit it again. "Send her in, Kate. And hold all my other calls."

A few moments later, the door opens and Casey steps in. Instantly my shitty mood elevates and I don't bother to hide my pleasure at seeing her again.

"Casey. This is a surprise."

She thanks Kate over her shoulder before the door closes behind her. Looking around nervously, she hugs the folder she's carrying to her chest.

"How have you been? Did you have a good holiday?"

She looks puzzled for a moment. "Holiday? Oh right. I didn't go home for Thanksgiving. My mom is a nurse and she usually volunteers to work that day so the people with families can stay home."

"Your mother sounds very kind."

The smile that covers her face is breathtaking. "My mom is the best." She holds out the folder. "I'm so sorry if I interrupted anything. I tried to tell your assistant that I was only here to drop this off."

My hand extends for the folder but really it's an excuse to get close to her again. There's something about being near her that just makes me happy.

That's what this is, I realize. This unexpected lightness, this buoyancy every time I see her. It's happiness. Clearly I didn't recognize it because it's been so long.

The folder contains the final markups from the first ad campaign. Jason has been asking for these. He's worried about the excess costs to change advertising at the last minute, so I asked Mya to finalize at least one ad that we could run at Fashion Week.

It has several panels, each with a model wearing a different outfit from our new line. There's a square representing the new Bridal division, the existing menswear line and then the first promo image from our new line of underwear.

"Thank you. I'll get this over to Jason immediately."

Casey smiles. "Mya might have mentioned that he was asking for it."

Which means Jason has also been making a nuisance of himself by calling the designers directly. "I'll have to ask his assistant to tighten his leash. He shouldn't be allowed to interact with too many people outside of the company."

Her eyes move around the room, taking in the mannequin in the corner and the board across from my desk where I keep all approved sketches for the next line. It inspires me to see what the rest of my design team has created and then I can design the central piece to complement them.

"Did you draw these?" She points at the board.

"Not all of them. This one is by Cristiane Laveque. She was just promoted this year to Creative Director. She's been with us since the inception of my menswear line."

I motion to the right side of the board where a rougher pencil sketch of a slinky evening dress is pinned.

"That's one of mine. One of the things I'm known for is mixing masculine and feminine elements so I decided to create evening wear for women. That's one of the reasons I employed Mirage, to help us change our image from a menswear brand, to an everyone brand."

"Maybe, if you're okay with it, we could use some sketches like these in some of the advertising."

"Like this one? It's just a quick pencil drawing. It's not even finished."

"I know! That's what makes it so cool." Her hands move as she talks, her excitement evident.

"I've never really thought about the whole process of how a design comes to life. But looking at this makes it seem really relatable, somehow. This drawing will then be turned into a pattern and created and then worn. If it's this interesting to me then I'm sure other people want to see it, too. People love behind the scenes stuff."

"Well, if you want to see what's really behind the scenes, I can show you around. You can actually see some of the junior designers at work creating sample pieces."

"Really. Right now?"

I laugh at her excitement. She's like a little kid with a new toy. "Of course. I have time if you don't need to get back."

She pulls out her phone. "I'm sure Mya won't mind. This is research after all."

Looking at her phone, I chuckle.

"What?"

"Just that after all that's happened, I still don't have your number."

She looks startled and then her cheeks redden. "Yeah, I guess we were a little busy that night. Here, put your number in before I call Mya."

As I type the digits in to a new contact on her phone, it feels like a small victory.

We spend the next hour walking through the design floor. Casey is interested in everything and stops frequently to compliment the designers on their work. Every time she does, I can see their chests puff up with pride. In just a quick tour, Casey has probably done more to fix company morale than anything my HR team has come up with.

Maybe Lavin Couture should try to hire her.

She tugs at my sleeve. "I hope I'm not keeping you from anything. I'm sure you didn't mean to spend this much time showing me around."

"I wouldn't have suggested it if I didn't have time. There's a board meeting soon so I was going to have to stop what I was doing anyway."

She frowns. "The stinky board that doesn't like recycling, you mean."

I smile at her description. Most of the members are old friends of my mother's and CEOs of other mega brands. Most are older and extremely conservative. It's not always easy to get approval for ideas that are new or different. But I'm used to dealing with the hassle. It's just part of my job.

When we turn the corner, I see Jason standing near the door with one of the members of the board.

"And this is our cue to get out of here." At her curious look, I motion discreetly with my head toward the door. "Jason is talking to one of the board members right now."

Casey's head swivels that way and then she gets a determined look in her eyes. Before I can process that, she's started walking.

"Jason, what a nice surprise! I didn't expect to see you today." Casey approaches Jason with an outstretched hand and a huge smile.

He looks startled, as am I, since I know they've only been introduced once. Her greeting makes it seem like they're good friends who chat all the time. He shakes her hand and then glances over at me with a *What the fuck?* expression but I just shrug. I have no idea what Casey is up to but I definitely want to find out.

"Nice to see you too, Miss Michaels."

Casey stares expectantly at the man next to him, and in the intervening silence it becomes clear she's waiting to be introduced.

"And this is Paul Nussbaum," Jason stammers finally. "There's a board of directors meeting today. Which means that we should probably head on—"

"Oh, you're on the board? How wonderful! Have you seen these samples yet?" Casey interrupts, linking her arm with Paul's and walking back toward the design floor.

He looks alarmed but there's not much he can do unless he wants to plant his feet and make her drag him. Casey starts pointing out various things to him and before long Paul is nodding and chuckling along with her.

"Well, I'll be damned. She's charmed that old goat, too."
Jason moves next to me, shaking his head as we follow behind.

"Don't start, Jason. She's a nice person."

"I didn't say she wasn't. I'll admit I was initially inclined
not to like her after watching you self-destruct for months.
But I can't hold that against her. It's not her fault you're a
sap."

I ignore that last comment as we come to where Casey
and Paul are watching one of the designers at work. We
approach in time to hear the tail end of what she's saying.

"Look at this beautiful fabric. It hurts to see so much of it
just land on the floor. But that's okay. I'm sure it's being recy-
cled in some way. Actually thank you for reminding me, Paul.
I meant to ask about Lavin Couture's green initiatives. We
need to highlight that in our campaign."

Paul looks back at us in confusion. "Green initiatives?"

"Oh yes, it's so important to be environmentally friendly
these days. People are tired of large companies that take from
Mother Earth but don't protect her. All it takes is one person
mentioning it on Twitter and the next thing you know your
company's name is trending for all the wrong reasons. But I
always pick up quite a few stocks on sale when that happens
so that's a plus."

Paul pales slightly. "Stocks on sale?"

Casey shrugs. "When that happens, the stock price of the

company in question usually nosedives. So I think of it like a sale."

He looks like he's going to be sick. "There *have* been some initiatives brought to the board's attention. They were just concerned about our fabric being used for inferior quality products. We don't want just anyone having Lavin quality goods."

Casey squeezes his arm conspiratorially. "Well, it's not like the fabric is what makes Lavin clothes so special. I'm sure other brands source fabric from the same places you do. What makes Lavin clothes so special is because they're designed by Andre, of course."

"And his fabulous team." She adds the last part in a loud voice that has several of the designers nearby grinning.

Paul is nodding along to every word she's saying now. "Green initiatives really are so important, aren't they? You know, the other board members can be a little slow to move with the times."

Casey pats his arm. "I'm sure you can convince them to do what's right. They'll listen to you, won't they?"

Paul beams. "Well, I am the chairman."

As they walk away, I can hear Casey's laughter. "I knew it. I could tell when I met you that you were a man of action."

Jason leans over. "Holy shit, did she just get your recycling plan on the board agenda? The woman is more dangerous than I thought."

16

Casey

I SPLASH WATER ON MY FACE AND PAT MY SKIN DRY WITH a paper towel. Talking for so long left my voice creaky and has given me a slight headache. Being the center of attention isn't my favorite thing but when Andre told me a board member was here, I knew this was a chance I wouldn't get again.

Paul actually turned out to be a nice man. A little stodgy and more moved by stock prices than people, but not a complete monster the way I'd imagined the board members must be. I mean, really? Who is against recycling? I figured most of them just hadn't thought about all of the positive sides to doing it.

I only wish I could have spent more time watching how Andre's company works but he had to get to his board meeting. And I've already been gone longer than I expected.

The door swings open behind me. An older woman enters and places her handbag on the counter next to mine. Her dark hair doesn't have a single strand of gray and her forehead is unlined. If I had to guess her age I would say she's one of those women who refuses to age past forty-five.

"So, you're the young woman causing so much commotion on the design floor today."

"I suppose I am. Hello." I'm not sure what she means about commotion but perhaps she's one of the designers I didn't get to meet. We did spend more than an hour down there talking to everyone. An unexpected interruption like that is probably a manager's nightmare.

"I apologize if your designers didn't get all their work done today. I was just so excited to see how they do it all."

I move over slightly and turn on the faucet. Hopefully that will keep us from having to blunder through any more polite conversation.

"My son seems to be quite taken with you."

I shut off the water.

My son. This cold, brittle woman is Andre's *mother?*

"It's not that I don't understand the allure. I once had a dalliance with the family gardener. He was a strapping man and quite a pleasure." The older woman meets my eyes in the mirror as she reapplies her lipstick. "But I'd already married and given my husband two sons. It was harmless and just as forgettable. My son hasn't yet done his duty."

Her eyes roam over my fitted skirt and blouse. She purses her lips as if unimpressed. A hot wave of embarrassment brings tears to my eyes.

The other woman pats my hand, her touch as cold as her eyes. "It's nothing personal, my dear. I'm sure you're a lovely young woman, but my son has responsibilities you can't begin to imagine. He needs someone appropriate for a man of his position. He'll be thirty soon and he's still unmarried. He needs to focus on his future."

I nod blindly although a petty part of me wants to tell her that he's only twenty-eight. That he's a grown man and can decide for himself what he wants. But I don't bother because in the end, none of it matters.

Andre and I … well, there is no Andre and I.

All we are is a catastrophe waiting to happen. Which is why we agreed to keep things professional in the first place.

"You have nothing to worry about, Mrs. Lavin. I'm just an employee of his marketing firm. Your son is a very nice man who agreed to give me a tour of the design floor today. I'm sure that once the marketing campaign is over I won't see him again." It hurts just to say the words but I need to hear them just as much as she does.

She drops her lipstick back into her bag and snaps it shut. "You're a sweet girl. You've eased a mother's heart today."

Two air kisses later she's gone, leaving a cloud of expensive perfume in her wake.

That's the kind of woman Andre grew up with. Even as I feel a shudder of sympathy, I envision the elegant women he's probably used to. Surely they aren't all this cold. One day, he'll meet someone warm and interesting who happens to have the right bloodline. Someone who'll fit in with his staunchly conservative mother and his exclusive social circle.

Someone *appropriate.*

It's only a matter of time before he has no reason to come back to DC. If we hadn't made an agreement to be friends, there's a chance we would have gotten caught up in the magic of how we feel and that would only make things harder in the end. The best thing I can do is forget what it felt like in his arms and concentrate on my own future. Maybe if I try hard enough, I can stop wishing for something that isn't good for me.

Luckily Mya is expecting me back in the office to help out with the design for another client. That'll cheer me up. I love assisting the designers because it allows me to see how the agency's core business operates. There are so many intricacies involved in developing a marketing plan, from the colors used in the advertising, to the radio and television coverage of the company's products.

After that *pleasant* little chat I need a pick-me-up.

I take a deep breath, resigned to brush off the negativity left from talking with Mrs. Lavin. Nothing the older woman said was a news flash. It's not like I didn't know all along our relationship couldn't work.

I just didn't expect the whole thing to depress me so much.

&

Traffic is horrendous which only adds to my grumpy mood as I make my way back to Mirage. I wave at Anya as I pass the reception desk, making a note to ask Mya about hiring some temporary help.

I was brought on to help out answering the phones so Anya didn't have to do it all the time. Now that I'm doing some marketing work as well, I feel bad that Anya is stuck behind that desk again along with all her work assisting James.

"Casey, there you are." Mya waves me in when I appear in the doorway to her office. "Close the door. I've already gotten started."

I take a seat in one of the chairs across from her. "Sorry I'm late. I was ... delayed."

Mya looks up. "Are you okay?"

"Oh yes. Fine. I just feel bad that Anya is stuck doing all

the receptionist work while I help out with this Lavin campaign."

She takes a deep breath. "I want to say something and I hope this isn't overstepping. But just because Mr. Lavin requested your help on this campaign doesn't mean you have to do it. I hope you aren't feeling pressured in any way."

"It's not like that!"

Mya grins. "Oh, so it's like *that*."

My head falls into my hand. "God, I hope I'm never interrogated by the police. I would crack before they even asked the first question."

"I'm not trying to be nosy but I just wanted to make sure things were on the up-and-up. Believe me, I'm not judging. He's a good-looking man."

"Won't James be upset if he finds out?"

Mya sniffs. "James would be a hypocrite if he did. He was married to someone he worked with and now he's with ... um, well. Now he's just bitter."

I'm pretty sure that wasn't what she was going to say but there's a chance she thinks I don't know about James and Anya.

"Well, at least I can tell Ariana it's not a secret anymore. I felt bad asking her to keep it from you. You're her best friend. I'm sure she tells you everything."

"Not everything," Mya says. "Ariana is a vault. That girl

has secrets upon secrets. I saw some things living in that apartment that I didn't even *want* an explanation for."

We both shudder. Some things shouldn't be remembered.

"Anyway, the point is that as long as you're happy, I'm happy. You've been a great help to me on this campaign and I think you have a lot of potential."

She pulls a sheaf of papers from her desk. She slaps them down on the desktop in front of me. "For the past two years, I've been pushing James to start an intern program. It makes more sense to hire people as interns while they're in college and then by the time they graduate, they're fully trained as marketing associates. If I can get him to agree, would you be interested?"

"Um, yeah. That would be amazing. But I'm not sure if I'm what he's looking for. I'm not really good with people."

Translation: I'm a tongue-tied introvert with fashion issues. Not exactly marketing associate material.

Marketing associates are always outgoing and sophisticated. They hobnob with the clients and convince them to trust their company's public profile to someone else. I never thought I'd actually be hired as a marketing associate for a place like this. I was expecting something less high-pressure. Maybe a marketing position for a chain store, where I'd be designing ad campaigns for batteries or shovels.

Mya lowers her voice. "I want to give you some advice. Something I wish someone had told me when I was younger."

She perches on the edge of her desk and picks up a picture frame. When she turns it, I can see it's a picture of Milo.

"I don't know if you're aware of this, but Milo and I have worked together for quite a while."

I shake my head. "I didn't know. It explains a lot, though. You two are so in sync it seems like you're reading each other's minds."

"Sometimes I think we *are* reading each other's minds. But things weren't always this way." She points at the picture. "Look at him. He looks like a runway model. He's always been like that, effortlessly gorgeous. Then there's me, the short, plump girl who couldn't even get a date in high school. I never thought he'd want me."

I watch wordlessly as Mya sets the photo back down. It's hard to believe what I'm hearing. This is gorgeous Mya Taylor, the woman all the men in the agency lust after. How can she not know that? Doesn't she notice the effect she has on others?

"Mya, you have the kind of figure that can stop traffic. Women pay money to have curves like yours."

"Well, thank you. But until I had the confidence to believe that, I pushed Milo away again and again. I almost lost him because I was too dumb to just believe what he told me." Mya looks at me pointedly. "And I really hope you aren't going to be as dumb as I was."

I bite my lip. "Mr. Lavin is an amazing man but we don't really have anything in common."

"I'm not just talking about Mr. Lavin. Despite what men seem to think, the world doesn't revolve around them. I'm talking about *you*, Casey. You have good instincts and an eye for what works. Take a chance, believe in yourself. Apply for the internship."

I shrug but a tickle of excitement creeps up my spine. "I don't know. I doubt I'd get it even if I applied. James probably won't want someone who has already dropped out of school once."

Mya sighs and walks back behind her desk. "You're just as dumb as I was. Which is probably why we get along so well." She claps her hands.

"Let's get to work on this Gemini ad. That's something we can tackle today."

17

Andre

As we finish up a meeting with our CFO, Jason makes a face behind his back like he's dying. This has been a day of never-ending meetings, one of my least favorite parts of the job. Gone are the days when I could sketch all day and sew all night. I cover a yawn with my hand.

After Casey's talk with Mr. Nussbaum on Monday, it took the board only twenty-four hours to review my prior proposal and approve it. One day. It would be hard to believe if I wasn't as firmly under her spell as everyone else.

Finally the meeting is over. Jason closes my office door

and collapses back against it. "Man, I thought he'd never leave."

"I hope nothing is wrong with the company because I wasn't paying any attention."

"That's why you have me to run shit around here. I'm actually surprised you've been around this week." He sits back down in the chair across from my desk.

There's nothing I can say to refute that since it's true. While I'm the CEO of the company, most CEOs rely heavily on their Chief Operating Officers to keep track of the different departments and make sure nothing goes wrong on a day-to-day basis.

"Where else would I be? It's only a month until Christmas, then it'll be New Year's. There's way too much work to do before the end of the year for me to take a vacation."

Jason smirks. "Not a vacation. I just figured you'd be spending *way* more time on marketing."

"Ah. Yes. Well, I haven't seen Casey since Monday."

He leans back in the chair and puts his hands on his head with a loud groan. "What the fuck are you doing, man? After all those months we couldn't find her, I thought you'd be all over things now. What the hell are you waiting for?"

While I can understand his confusion, it still irritates me to hear him talk about her like that. Like she's just some conquest or some chick I want to screw again.

"She's focused and determined to make her mark in her career. I'm trying to respect her wishes. What do you want me to do, go stalk her when she's made it clear she just wants to be friends?"

He looks chagrined. "Okay, I get it. But you can at least tell her that she saved the day with the board. Isn't that a friend thing? At least give her the credit for that."

I still have to get a budget approved for how much we can spend on repurposing the scrap material into garments to donate, but the hardest part is over. She accomplished something I've been trying to get done for a long time. Casey is the entire reason that Lavin Couture now has a recycling program.

She definitely deserves the credit.

"I'm willing to admit you have a point. Now get out of here so I can figure out how to tell her that."

He leaves with a mocking bow and I then turn to look at my phone with trepidation. She's still at work so maybe I shouldn't call her now. When I entered my number on her phone, I made sure to text myself so I'd have hers. It's been so tempting seeing that message sitting in my texting app. It would be so easy to reply to it, to initiate a conversation about something related to the campaign just for the excuse of claiming some of her time.

But each time I stop myself, worried that I'm doing the

exact thing I told myself I wouldn't do: pressure her for more than she wants to give.

However this time Jason is right. I have legitimate business news that she deserves to hear. Finally I curse my own indecision and hit her name to call her.

"Hello?"

"Casey. It's Andre."

"I know." She sounds like she's whispering. "I was just surprised to hear your voice. Is everything okay? Do you need me to get Mya?"

"No, I called for you. Good news: the board approved the recycling program."

After a pause, Casey erupts into a muffled squeal. "Holy crap, seriously? That's great. I mean, I figured Paul would come through for us but you can never be sure about these things."

Why is he Paul? Disgruntled, I remember how long she insisted on calling me Mr. Lavin even though it was completely unnecessary but she meets Nussbaum once and suddenly he's Paul?

"It's all thanks to you. You're the one who convinced *Mr. Nussbaum* to vote yes on the proposal. Where he goes the others usually follow."

"It was the right thing. I'm just thrilled they actually agreed."

"So we should celebrate. Dinner tonight?"

"Um ... you don't have to do that. It was no big deal."

"Our company will have a smaller carbon footprint and some of DC's residents will have warm clothing this winter thanks to you. It's a very big deal."

I can hear the smile in her voice when she responds. "Thanks. It feels good to be a part of something that matters. I guess we could do dinner."

"Good. I'll pick you up from work. Unless you'd rather go home first. I could pick you up at your apartment."

"No! Don't do that." Casey coughs. "At work is fine. See you then."

After we hang up, I sit back with a satisfied smile. This is probably the only time such a lackluster acceptance has ever made me feel so good. With Casey, I've had to work for every inch and even though this is just a friendly dinner, it feels more important than any other date I've ever had.

Right before five o'clock, I pull up in front of the Madison building and put the car in park to wait.

I love the energy of Washington, DC. There are always people rushing by in dark suits or joggers with their dogs. It's a city that never sleeps but with a totally different vibe than New York or Los Angeles. In New York the energy is manic, so much going on that I feel drugged every second I'm there. Los Angeles feels like moving through a dream with its loud colors and obsession with physical beauty.

The nation's capital is just as vibrant but with a controlled pace and an orderly energy. Here the celebrities are senators and congressmen instead of actors and musicians. It reminds me more of Milan although it can't touch Italian architecture. I'm definitely biased.

Fifteen minutes after five, Casey pushes open the building's glass doors and steps out onto Connecticut Avenue.

I watch as she looks both ways and then starts walking in the opposite direction. I lower the window slightly and whistle at her. She turns and glares at the car before turning her attention back to her phone.

Lowering the window all the way, I lean out. "Cassandra, don't be difficult."

She whirls around at the sound of her name. "Andre! I thought you were going to call me before you got here."

As soon as she gets in and shuts the door I pull back into traffic.

"I figured you were getting off soon anyway, so I decided to just wait. Why didn't you come over at first?"

She laughs. "Because you *whistled* at me, you jerk. I thought you were some random guy hitting on me. It happens occasionally. Men in this city will hit on anything that moves. Well, I suppose men are like that in every city."

I can only imagine. When I whistled at her I was being playful, never considering that it might come across as disrespectful. Not that I'm unaware those things happen but she speaks about it as just a fact of life. And for her it is—a sobering thought. Maybe I should pick her up from work everyday.

When the car rolls to a smooth stop at a red light, the people in the next car do a double take.

"Why are people staring? They can't see us, can they?" Casey squints as she peers though the tinted window.

"It's the car. Bugattis always draw attention. I decided to have it shipped since I'll be here for a while."

"*Bugatti*. Sounds fancy."

I decide not to tell her that a Bugatti Veyron is about two million dollars' worth of fancy. Philippe will definitely get a kick out of this conversation later.

"Anyway, all I know about cars is they're expensive to buy, expensive to fuel and expensive to park. I was excited when I learned that most city dwellers don't bother with them. I left my old car back at home. It's so old it probably wouldn't have survived the trip anyway." Casey leans her head back against the headrest with a weary sigh.

"Tired?"

"A little."

"We can stay in. I'll get something delivered. What do you feel like for dinner? Italian, French or maybe Chinese?"

"I can't imagine you eating moo shu pork from a little white box." Casey grins over at me. "Now I'm tempted to ask for Chinese just to see what you would order."

"I like all types of food." I pull into the underground parking of my building and punch in the security code to gain access. After we park, I round the car to open her door. She takes my hand and allows me to pull her to her feet.

"I'm actually curious about what you eat most of the time. Do you even know how to cook?"

I take the teasing in stride. If I hadn't had my father's influence, there's a good chance that I'd be as spoiled and sheltered as she probably assumes.

"Prepare to be amazed, *signorina*. Tonight I am going to prepare my signature dish. I only prepare it for treasured guests a few times a year so you are in for a treat."

Casey plays along, squeezing my arm as we ride the elevator to the top floor. "Do tell. I can't wait to be amazed."

When the elevator doors open, I gesture for her to walk out first. "Go ahead and get comfortable. The remote is next to the couch if you want to watch some TV."

Casey slips off her shoes, leaving them next to the front door. "I'll hang out with you in the kitchen. It's not often I get to see a master chef at work."

I get ready to cook. First, I wash my hands and then tuck a dish towel in the front of my slacks to protect them from splatter. Then, I pour Casey a glass of wine and another for myself. She sits at the counter in the kitchen watching as I arrange my ingredients. I set out bread, cheese, butter and a few spices. Then I reach below to retrieve a cast iron skillet.

I gesture at it all with a flourish. "Get ready for the best damn grilled cheese you've ever had!"

Casey giggles as I spread butter across the pieces of bread before layering them with thick slices of smoked cheddar cheese. "Grilled cheese. That's your masterpiece? Well, I have to admit you really look like you know what you're doing. I'm impressed."

I place the first sandwich in the skillet with a generous dollop of butter.

"My father came from humble beginnings. But unlike a lot of people we know, he never tried to hide it. He refused to let anyone treat it as a weakness. Instead he made it a strength. If I'm even half the man he was, I'll be happy. He passed away five years ago and there are days I still pick up the phone to call him before I remember."

She smiles sadly. "I'm so sorry. I bet he was so proud of you."

"He was. And of my younger brother Philippe. My mother is proud of us as well, I know she is; she just has a different way of showing that."

"Oh yeah, your mother. We met."

Her words make me jerk and my elbow hits my glass of

wine, sending it flying. The sound of the glass shattering seems so loud. For a moment I can't move. Can't breathe.

"Andre? Are you okay?"

I can hear her calling my name but I can't respond. Then in a sudden rush, I'm back. I move forward on shaky feet and turn off the burner with a flick of my wrist.

"Sorry about that." My hands are shaking as I go to the pantry and retrieve a broom. Embarrassed by my extreme reaction, I wonder how I'll explain this to Casey. "I'm probably not good company right now. Maybe we can get a rain check on dinner?"

Warm fingers cover mine, startling me. "I don't want to go unless you don't want me here anymore. And you don't have to apologize. I'm not sure what just happened but I can see that something shook you. The same thing happened at the Preview Gala with that woman. When she hugged you, you looked like you'd just seen a ghost."

"Something happened. Earlier this year. I don't really talk about it."

Warm brown eyes meet mine. "Well then we won't."

With gentle fingers she takes the broom and sweeps the glass into a small pile in the corner.

"That's it? You don't want to know what happened?"

She takes me by surprise when she shakes her head. "Not if talking about it makes you remember it again. If you want to tell me, I want to listen. But until then, I plan on relaxing with my friend and eating the dinner he made for me."

I watch as she walks back to the stovetop and uses the spatula to flip the sandwich onto the plate, revealing a golden brown underside. She picks it up and takes a big bite.

"You know, I almost don't want to admit it but this *is* the best damn grilled cheese I've ever had."

18

Casey

WE SPEND THE REST OF THE EVENING EATING GRILLED cheese sandwiches and arguing about what to watch on TV. Andre wants to watch a documentary on Netflix that sounds boring as hell while I want to watch a new baking show.

We compromise by watching a home decorating show.

The entire time I'm watching him carefully for signs of trouble. Even though I told him I don't want to talk about what happened, maybe that was a mistake. Is it healthier for him to talk about it? Could I be doing him more harm than good by letting him pretend his episode in the kitchen earlier didn't happen?

Truly, I don't know and the answers are too important.

Andre looks at me then and smiles. "Thank you for staying with me. I wouldn't have thought this would help but it did."

His words only make me feel worse.

"I didn't do anything. Just watched a show. I wish I knew what else to do to help you."

He's quiet for a moment. "Earlier this year, a young girl stabbed herself on the red carpet of a movie premiere I was attending. We don't know much, but it's thought she did it to prove her love to me."

My hand slowly comes up to cover my mouth. "Oh no. How terrible."

"Yes, it was. Terrible that a young girl almost lost her life because of me."

I put a gentle hand on his cheek. "This has to feel personal. But I'm sure you know this really wasn't about you."

His eyes close briefly. "It was my name she was screaming over and over. It was my Instagram page that inspired her. We did a Halloween image where I'm wearing fake blood on my shirt. The caption read, *My heart bleeds just for you. Who would you bleed for?*"

"And if she'd seen another celebrity's page that day, she might have chosen to hurt herself in a different fashion. It sounds like that was a cry for help and she latched on to anyone she could relate to in some way."

He doesn't respond and my heart breaks watching him struggle with his thoughts. But I have a feeling there's more, so I wait.

"We kept it as quiet as possible to discourage copycats. But after that day, I started having panic attacks. That's what that was in the kitchen."

He blinks several times. I pretend not to notice the moisture in the corners of his eyes.

"Now you know. It's only fair you tell me your deepest secret, you know."

He's joking, trying to bring this conversation back to a lighter place but something inside me doesn't want to shrug this off.

"People always talk about women having it all, meaning career and family. But a lot of times what they really mean is career first and kids later. But that's actually not what I want. I would love to have a baby first."

He's watching me so closely that I shift uneasily. That's probably not the sexiest thing to admit to a guy. Well, if I wanted him to keep me in the friend zone, that's the way to do it. Nothing like talk of children and commitment to send most guys running.

"My only serious boyfriend in college, Thad, seemed to understand. He made me feel beautiful. He was a grad student and seemed so sophisticated compared to anyone else I knew. But he always had a reason to explain why I couldn't see him on the weekends. I ignored my gut feelings when he would cancel plans and turned a blind eye to all the signs he was a liar."

"He disappointed you."

I nod. "Yes. It turns out he already had my dream life with another woman. His wife had the babies with him I'd been dreaming of."

"He was a fool." Andre squeezes my fingers. "And I won't pretend I'm sorry about that. Because I don't know what I would have done if I'd met you when you were married to someone else." He looks at me with probing eyes. "That's your deepest secret? That you want to have a baby?"

I sigh. "It might not seem like a big deal to you but my mom had me young. The people in our hometown treated her like an outcast. Small towns can be a great place to grow up but they can also be a harsh place if you do something they don't approve of. Being a pregnant, single, college-dropout was definitely not something they approved of. I can *never* tell my mom I want to have a baby young. Having me ruined her life."

"That can't be true," he argues. "I'm sure she would agree that you are the best thing she's ever done."

The words warm me. My mom used to always tell me that when I was a little girl.

"How did you know she used to say that?"

"Simple. I'm looking at you."

While my heart is busy exploding at his sweet words, he turns and I can feel the rush of his breath on my cheek. Now that the sun has gone down it's dark in the room, the only light coming from the television.

My mind is telling me to do one thing and my body is crying out for me to throw myself into his arms. And it's getting harder to pretend I only care about him as a friend.

His lips feather gently over my eyes, cheeks and then finally, *finally,* my mouth.

I clasp his shirt in my fists and pull him closer. With a stark, animal sound, his hands settle on my lower back as we kiss, only breaking apart to take desperate, greedy breaths. His taste explodes on my tongue, heady like sandalwood, cinnamon and man.

It's too much at once, too many sensations to process.

He groans and the sound is almost swallowed up by the desperate way our mouths connect. "You don't know what you do to me."

"I don't want to be just friends," I admit in a rush of breath. It feels good to say it aloud.

"Tell me what you do want, baby." Andre skims a finger over my cheek. "You know you have only to ask."

At the husky timbre of his voice, my nipples tighten. His finger trails down my neck and over the swell of one breast. This has to be a dream, a wine-fueled hallucination. But if this is a dream, it can't hurt to ask for one thing.

"I want you. I don't think I've ever wanted anything more."

Andre moves so quietly in the dark, his breath warm on my neck as he embraces me. His scent overwhelms my senses and I react instinctively, curling against him.

He growls, the arm around my waist tightening until I can't move. He holds my gaze, unblinking, as he lowers his head and I just *melt* into a puddle of lust, my mouth open against his.

He lifts me into his arms easily and carries me down the hallway to the bedroom I've never seen. It's too dark to see much until he turns on a low light next to the bed. Then I don't care what the room looks like because he lowers himself on top of me.

My hands travel over the flat planes of his chest and around to his back, which tenses as my fingers move over him. He's hard everywhere, his arms like steel cages locking me in place. His lips glide over my cheek to torment the skin on my throat.

I wiggle out of the tight skirt I wore today and then unbutton my blouse. When my plain black bra comes into view, I send up a silent prayer that it's in decent shape and not one of my bras with a weird design on it.

Not that I think Andre would even notice. He unhooks the back deftly and pushes the cups out of the way so he can take a taut nipple in his mouth. I bite my lip to stifle a wild cry.

"You don't have to hide the sounds of your pleasure. I want to hear what my touch does to you."

"It makes me feel like I'm on fire." It's not an exaggeration. His lips burn against my skin, putting every nerve ending at attention.

His dark head moves back and forth between the tips of my breasts, alternately sucking and biting on them. I never knew I could feel these sensations, never guessed at the amount of passion untapped within me. The things he's doing with his tongue make me want to crawl out of my skin and all over him. I want him inside me and all over me.

I never want him to stop.

When I look down, the sight of his arm moving between my thighs pulls a whimper from my lips. He hooks a finger through the edge of my panties and pulls them to the side. I cry out, first in surprise then in pleasure.

"I knew you'd be wet for me. I have to feel you." One long finger sinks deep and we both moan at the decadent sensation.

There's something primal about having one leg cocked over his hip while his hand plays between my legs. He shifts, the base of his palm rubbing directly against my clit. The heat builds with every press of his finger and grind of his palm. I shift my hips, unconsciously tilting up with the rhythm of his hand.

"You're so tight, so perfect." He mutters something in Italian before capturing my lips in a drugging kiss. "*Cara*, you make me want." His accent is thicker now, his control obviously gone.

That I've caused him to be in this state feels incredibly satisfying, especially when I reach down and unzip his pants, gently palming the evidence of his excitement. His length presses long and thick in my hand. His head falls back as I stroke him. He fumbles in the nightstand next to the bed, pulling out a condom. He stands and pushes his slacks down before reaching over his head to yank off his shirt.

It's almost embarrassing that he was still fully dressed while I'm completely naked.

I watch with greedy eyes as he rolls the protection on, my desire building with every breath. Some hazy part of me acknowledges that this is probably a bad idea but I just want one more night where we can be Andre and Casey without worrying about all the rest.

He kisses me again, his tongue invading my mouth as our bodies align. Then he lifts one of my legs, holding it around his waist as he angles his hips. I'm so wet that I take him all the way in one thrust.

Something dark and intense passes over his face. His beautiful eyes take it all in as I move under him, rocking my hips until we're moving together in the perfect rhythm. One hand comes to his face as I whisper his name over and over. I thought I remembered how good it was but I'm unprepared for how emotional it makes me feel.

The orgasm takes me by surprise, heat spreading from my toes, up through my core and radiating out, tingling even the tips of my ears.

I squeeze my eyes shut at the soul-crushing wave of pleasure. Andre moans into my mouth as he comes. We rest like that, all our limbs entwined as our hearts slow.

"I've never felt like this about anyone before." I bury my face against his shoulder at the admission, suddenly very self-conscious.

Andre anchors my face with a strong hand and kisses me again. "And if I have my way, you never will. You are mine."

When I open my eyes, it takes me a second to remember where I am. Then I turn my head and see Andre and it all comes back. My mind is still hazy with dreams and I don't have the mental energy to remember that I'm not supposed to get attached to him.

Maybe for just a few minutes this morning I can allow myself to imagine what it would be like to have this life. Waking up with a man who treats me like his queen. Children in the other room that are the perfect blend of both of us.

It seems like it would be a fairy tale. But here in the quiet moments before I'm fully awake, it's okay to indulge in the dream.

Then Andre lets out a loud snore and I have to cover my giggles with the comforter. Maybe fairy tales aren't so unrealistic after all. I bet even Prince Charming snores sometimes.

"What are you over there laughing about?"

He has a rough morning voice, nothing like the cultured tones I'm used to hearing. And how much do I love that I get to know this about him?

"Just over here listening to you sawing logs."

His puzzled expression only makes it funnier.

"You know, sawing logs. Snoring."

He props himself up with one arm. "What an odd expression. It seems whenever I think my English is pretty good, I get proven wrong." He looks over to the digital clock on the nightstand. "I should get you home so you can change before work."

I grumble a little, not ready for the spell to be broken. "Can't we just play hooky? Let's pretend we're back in high school. I can fake a pretty good cough and pretend to be sick."

"That sounds way more fun than what I have planned this morning. But no way. I refuse to be a bad influence on you. Plus, if something interesting happens at work you'll be upset you missed it."

Reluctantly, I stand and pull my panties on. He's right and irritatingly so. It would be just my luck that Mya had some cool project planned for a day I called in sick.

"Okay but I don't understand why you're suddenly afraid of corrupting me. I'm pretty sure you weren't worried about that last night."

He grins evilly. "No. And I won't be worried about it tonight either."

That's almost enough to make me want to take the panties back off.

"Focus. Focus. Focus." I get my clothes back on, while admiring his naked ass as he moves around the room. He disappears into his closet and then comes back out fully dressed.

"No fair. You look like James Bond and I have to do the walk of shame in my wrinkled clothes from yesterday."

He leans over and plants a kiss on my forehead. "You're welcome to leave clothes here. That should make it fair, hmm?"

"Really?" The thought makes me a little giddy but also introduces so many questions. What are we doing? Are we a couple now? I don't want to be the typical clingy girl asking for meaning when maybe he was just lonely and in the moment yesterday. But to me, it felt like we said some pretty significant things last night.

I'm just not sure how they hold up in the light of day.

"You have the most expressive face. I can see everything you're thinking." He chuckles and pulls me into his arms.

I relax against his chest. "Was yesterday a dream?"

"No. At least I hope not because I felt like it was the start of something pretty special. I know you're worried about what will come but all I ask is for a chance to prove myself."

"You don't have anything to prove." Doesn't he get it? He's already got me. He's the one I want and I've only been fooling myself to think we could be just friends this long.

"I want to do this right. I want to take you to dinner. Hold your hand. Listen to you complain about your boss when you've had a bad day. All of it."

My heart is dancing hearing him describe everything I've ever wanted. But as usual, reality intrudes.

"I want all those things you described but I'm worried about what happens when the campaign is over. We live very different lives. You're a rich, famous guy and I'm a small-town girl. It feels like a fairy tale now but what happens when the clock strikes twelve?"

He shakes his head. "You're right that we're different. But different doesn't mean impossible."

I feel like he's deliberately missing my point. "Can you

really see me at one of your fashion shows? On the red carpet with you? I don't fit into your world."

"My world is what I make it. I can give that all up and live happily for the rest of my life on the money I already have."

"That's not what I want. You enjoy your work just like I do. I would never want you to give that up for me."

Andre leans his forehead against mine. When we're together like this, it's so easy to forget about the outside world. But that world is always going to be there.

Doesn't he understand that I'm just trying to protect the both of us? I know what it feels like to be heartbroken and humiliated. It's funny, even though he's the one in the public eye, he doesn't understand how vicious people can be when you fall from grace. I do.

"We tried to be just friends and I don't know about you, but I was miserable. We did things backward from the start so lets try something different. Spend the next few days with me. Go to work and be the amazing career woman that you are. But then spend your evenings with me. Get to know me and let me get to know you."

"You want to date?"

He leans back and looks me dead in the eye. "I want to be the man in your life. The one who won't let you down."

19

Andre

EVEN THOUGH SHE LETS IT GO, I CAN TELL SHE'S STILL worried. But her expressive face revealed her true secrets as she told me about the asshole she dated in college. What happened to her may be different from what happened to her mother, but I'm sure it felt much the same. To be abandoned by someone you trusted and treated like you aren't good enough would make anyone wary.

I don't want her to ever feel that way again.

Like I told her, things have been backward from the start with us. Sex, then friendship, then sex. But it's important to me that I show her she matters. That the way we started isn't going to determine how our relationship ends. That she can count on me to be honest and to stick around.

I know there will be some hard times ahead. People who won't be happy to see us together and I'm sure my mother will be at the top of that list. But none of those things should keep two people who care about each other apart. I plan to spend the next few days showing her how a man is supposed to treat the lady in his life.

She deserves that.

As we agreed, Friday after work Casey comes directly to the penthouse.

"Hey. How was your day?"

"Excellent. I got you something for our date Saturday night." I go back to my room and then come back carrying the dress carefully.

"You didn't," she breathes.

"I did. It's a sample gown I had altered by one of the junior designers. You'll be the first to wear a dress from our new evening wear line. I'm taking you to the symphony tomorrow night."

There's a heated look in her eyes as she undresses right there in the living room. As she steps into the dress, it flows over her curves like water.

"You look like a princess."

Casey blushes prettily. "I feel like one, too. So I guess that makes you my Prince Charming. I can't wait to wear this Saturday!"

The next day seems to drag but finally it's Saturday night and we arrive at the symphony. I enjoy watching her reactions to everything. Her eyes are alight with discovery at the lush interior of the Kennedy Center and the swirl of gowns and tuxedos.

"This is so exciting. I feel like I'm in a movie," she whispers as we take our seats.

She falls asleep ten minutes into the performance.

And I fall in love with her just as fast.

We spend the rest of the night watching television on the couch and eating ice cream straight from the carton. I carry her to bed and make love to her like we have forever. Then I watch her as she sleeps and wonder if the incredible luck I've had in my life will continue long enough for me to make her mine.

The next day, Casey asks if she can plan a date. We're eating pancakes she made from scratch. She looks adorable with mussed hair and pancake batter on her cheek. It's a view that I hope I'll be seeing every Sunday from now on.

"You're doing the whole gentlemanly, *let-me-treat-you-right* thing, and I love it. But I'm dying to take you somewhere in particular so please say yes."

As if I could deny her anything. "Okay. Where are we going?"

I'm ready to pretend to enjoy a chick flick when she says, "It's a surprise. Actually, did you finish sewing that sample pair of your activewear trousers?" At my nod, she wiggles with delight. "Good. Wear those."

"Now I'm really curious."

She keeps me in suspense the entire time as we ride the metro. Then proceeds to take me to a laser tag place and kick my ass at the game.

I've never had so much fun.

But when I arrive home from work on Monday evening, I have to admit my favorite part has been this. The quiet evenings spent together. With her laptop, she can do work from home and I've quickly become accustomed to the sound of her typing away in the background as I sketch or review financial reports.

Spending time with her doing nothing is the greatest joy. Well, not nothing. This is us, after all.

I take off my suit jacket as I approach the couch. Casey is curled up on the sofa watching television. I lean over and nuzzle her neck. My phone dings in my pocket. I ignore it. I nip her shoulder just as the chirping sound starts again.

"You should probably answer that." Casey's husky laugh flows over me, the sexy sound making me hard instantly.

"It can wait."

"It's okay. If it's business you should take care of it. I really should be studying anyway. I have a statistics quiz in two days." But she doesn't move away as I continue sampling the soft skin on her neck.

Then my phone rings. Again.

I groan. Apparently whoever it is won't give up until I answer.

She rises gracefully and stretches, the hem of her shirt rising to show the curve of her back. I lean over and grab for her, intent on pulling her back into my arms.

"No way, mister. I have schoolwork to do." She picks up her laptop from the sofa next to her and walks toward the bedroom.

"Damn, you make it hard for me to think about work." I pull out my phone, already annoyed at whoever it is.

There are two calls from my mother. Those can definitely wait. There's one call from my brother. I hit the button to return the call. He answers on the first ring.

"Please call Mamma. You know how she gets when you ignore her," Philippe pleads.

"You just don't want to deal with her." I laugh at the exasperated snort that comes through the line.

"I've been dealing with her. Who do you think she complains to about you spending so much time with an *Americana*? Next thing I know, she'll turn all that attention on me. I hope this rebellion of yours has been worth it. I'm pretty sure she's planning a full-scale attack to marry you off as soon as you come back."

I walk into the bedroom. The light is on in the bathroom and I can hear the shower. My mind helpfully supplies an image of Casey standing under the streaming water, her profusion of dark curls hanging in ropy, wet tendrils down her bare back. My desire for her is almost frightening in its intensity. I've been with beautiful women before, probably more than my share, but I've never *craved* a woman this way.

"It's been more than worth it. There's a chance I may not come back, little brother." My statement is met with stunned silence.

Finally Philippe says, "I won't pretend I understand but I'm happy for you. She must be quite a woman." He sounds bewildered by the idea of settling down but at least I have his support.

I wouldn't have thought I needed or wanted anyone's approval but knowing my brother is on my side makes me feel a lot better. Especially since I'm sure my mother is going to make my life hell before she accepts my decision to move to the States and live with an unknown American woman.

"She's amazing. The kind of woman I didn't even know existed. Do me a favor though and don't mention what I said about moving, *per favore*? The last thing I need is Mamma to find out and start her scheming. You know how she is. They already met once and I'm sure it wasn't pleasant. I won't subject Casey to her sharp tongue if I can help it."

I wish I could somehow exempt myself from Mamma's

criticism too but at least I've had a lifetime of experience in ignoring it. Someone as softhearted as Casey would be in tears in minutes.

"She had Marcella over for dinner the other night. You know what that means. She's still upset that you broke the engagement. But I'll do what I can to distract her. I don't want to see her ruin this for you."

"No worries, little brother. I'm never getting back with Marcella or any of the other women she's thrown at me. That was five years ago and Mamma is going to have to learn to accept it. I'm a grown man. There's nothing she can do to ruin this for me. "

⚓

A few minutes later when Casey emerges from the bathroom, I'm still thinking about my conversation with Philippe. I told him that I'm in this for the long haul and there's nothing that can ruin this. But there is something. Our tendency to dance around issues instead of facing them head on. So I decide to ask about something that's been bothering me.

"Why haven't I seen your apartment?"

Casey pauses in the act of putting her underwear on. Then she slowly starts inching it up her legs, finally pulling it into place with a little snap.

"Stop trying to distract me."

"I'm *not*. I just didn't think you'd want to see my little apartment when you live in this palace."

"I want to know everything about you."

She smiles at that. "My roommate is a little strange. Mya described her to me as *kooky* when we first met and I have to say, I haven't found a better word to describe her yet."

"I'm used to creative types. I'm sure your *kooky* friend isn't anything I can't handle. The depravity in the world of the megarich isn't an exaggeration, unfortunately. It would be pretty hard to shock me."

Casey looks skeptical but then shrugs as if she's resigned to whatever happens. "Well, if you're sure. Let's sleep there tonight then."

That wasn't what I meant but I'm not taking it back. If this is my only opportunity to see Casey's world, then I'm there. Even if it means sleeping on a smaller bed with a roommate one wall away.

Casey warns me there's very little street parking, so we take a cab to her place. I've brought a small bag with a change of clothes and a toothbrush. But once we're walking up the stairs, Casey's steps get slower and slower.

"What's wrong? Did you forget something?"

She whirls around. "Ariana is really pretty. Am I stupid for introducing you to my gorgeous, crazy, fun roommate?"

"You're not stupid. But it's cute that you think I'll actually notice anyone else but you. Remind me to tell you about all the times I went back to the bar where we met. I'm pretty sure the bartender thought I was a stalker. They probably have my picture up in the back."

She takes a deep breath. "That's really sweet. But also kinda creepy."

We continue up the stairs to the third floor and Casey pulls her keys out. She unlocks a door in the middle of the hall but the door won't open more than a few feet.

"Hold on. Ariana left the chain on the door. She probably assumed I wasn't coming back for the night." She knocks and a few minutes later, we hear the sound of the door being unlatched.

The young woman who opens the door of the apartment is beautiful. Casey wasn't exaggerating about that. But she's obviously very suspicious since she only pokes her head out.

When she notices Casey, she grins. "Oh, its just you."

Then she opens the door all the way and I see that she's wearing a baby carrier. Which is odd because Casey didn't mention her roommate having a baby. Then I jump back.

"*Merda*! What the hell is that?"

The baby in her carrier is a gnarled, grizzly-looking thing. Like a cross between a werewolf and a teddy bear.

Ariana looks down. "Oh, that's just Edward. Come on in."

I glance back at Casey who just shrugs and follows her roommate inside. I walk in, inching around the crazy girl with the demon wolf baby around her neck. The apartment is small but cozy. Even though it's my first time here, I can definitely see Casey's influence. There's a stack of books on the table next to the couch.

Now that Casey spends so much time at the penthouse, I find books everywhere. In the living room. In the kitchen. I even found a book in the pantry once. I can only guess that she was reading it while getting a snack and accidentally set it down in there.

"Ariana. This is Andre." Casey's eyes drop to the baby carrier. "And we're not even going to ask about that."

"No. We're asking about that," I interrupt.

Ariana hefts the "baby" up higher, adjusting it in the carrier. "This is my metro buddy. Whenever I have the night shift, I carry Edward with me. It keeps people from talking to me or sitting too close on the metro. You'd be surprised how much personal space weirdness buys you."

Casey sighs. "That shouldn't make that much sense. But this is one of the least weird things I've seen you do since I moved here so ... yeah. Good night!"

Ariana waves as she leaves.

Once the door shuts behind her, we both burst into laughter.

"So that's your roommate."

Casey grabs me by the hand and leads me down a hallway. "She's one of the strangest people I've ever met but also one of the nicest. And as a bonus, I feel really safe living with her. I'm not sure too many people would willingly tangle with her."

We enter the room on the left and I look around curiously. The room is plain but feminine with a towering stack of pillows on the bed. There's another pile of books next to the bed. While I'm putting my bag down I notice Casey slipping one of the books into the nightstand drawer.

"Whoa. What was that?"

She blushes. "Just a dirty book that I don't want you to see, okay?"

I love that she's so shy about that kind of thing. You'd think after everything we've done together that it wouldn't even bother her.

"This is where you were sleeping all those nights we were apart. Do you know how many times I imagined you out there in the world somewhere? Wondered if you were safe, loved and if you knew how much our short time together meant to me? And all the while you were here, sharing an apartment with a woman who has a demon baby doll."

Tears are in her eyes as she hugs me around the waist. "I'm here now. We're here now. Together. And that's how it's going to stay."

20

Casey

"WE NEED SOME HELP WITH THE DESIGN BOARDS FOR the Anderson Project." Mya ticks off points on the fingers of her left hand on Friday morning while I halfheartedly scribble notes on a yellow legal pad. "Also, we have an internal staff meeting scheduled for this afternoon."

I nod and cover my yawn with the back of my hand. I'm having trouble keeping my eyes open. Andre had to fly back to Italy unexpectedly because his mother became ill. Even though she wasn't very nice to me, I don't blame him for wanting to spend time with her and make sure she's feeling better. He's already lost one parent which is a pain that I wouldn't wish on anyone.

Which is why I felt even worse turning him down when he asked me to come with him. He said he understood but that was in the middle of packing a bag in a rush.

We've been texting every night but it's not the same. This isn't the kind of thing I feel comfortable talking about on a transatlantic phone call. But the tension between us and getting used to being back in my own bed has led to four days of sleepless nights.

"I'll be conducting a follow-up session with Indigo Jewelers in about thirty minutes that I could use your assistance with. Then after that we could go dance naked on 18th Street."

I nod again before the words sink in. "Wait, what?"

Mya laughs. "You've barely heard a word I've said. Where is your mind this morning? Or should I even ask?"

"I'm sorry. I haven't been sleeping too well. I've never been so happy to see the weekend arrive."

I follow Mya out into the hall. Milo is outside talking to Wallace, one of the junior associates. We've been working all morning and I'm more than ready to break for lunch. The couch that Mya just got for her office was calling out to me.

"I have a meeting with Milo right now so I'll see you after lunch, Casey." Mya stops suddenly. "Mr. Lavin! We weren't expecting you today."

My head snaps up. Andre is standing right in front of the reception desk.

"There was a change of plans," he responds softly.

Everything inside me wants to run over and jump into his arms. But I can't do that with all these people around. So even though I'm mentally screaming, I just say, "Hey."

"Hey to you, too." His eyes shift briefly to the side and I know he's struggling not to say anything that could get me in trouble.

Mya gives me a wink. "I'll let Mr. Lawson know you want a meeting. Casey, why don't you show Mr. Lavin to whatever conference room is available."

I nod, grateful for the direction. My mind isn't exactly working properly right now. All I can see is that my man is back in town and I really want to jump him. "Please follow me, Mr. Lavin."

The first conference room we pass is empty so I take him there. Even if someone else is scheduled to use the room, I'll juggle the schedule around. Anything is better than standing in the hallway with my lover who I'm pretending is just a client.

As soon as we clear the doorframe, Andre pulls me into his arms. "What have I told you about that Mr. Lavin thing?"

I inhale, taking in his scent. "You know why I'm doing that. We have to be professional while we're in the office."

His hand tightens on my back. "It is pretty sexy, especially when you're wearing that skirt. You know I like that one. Maybe I should have you call me Mr. Lavin at home, sometimes."

"Mr. Lavin. How unexpected!"

At the sound of James's voice, we spring apart. I take the opportunity to duck out, ignoring Andre's scowl.

I march down the hallway at a fast clip until I reach the ladies' restroom. At least he can't follow me in here.

"That's what you think. Do you know that you talk to yourself when you're nervous?" His face appears in the mirror over my shoulder.

"What are you doing? This is the *ladies'* room."

He kisses the side of my neck and just like that my panties are flooded. I fight back the desire already curling through my veins. With him, the slightest touch can send me over the edge. Just a look and I'm dripping wet and ready for him. If it didn't feel so good, it would be painful.

"I came straight here from the airport." Andre closes his eyes as he speaks and I can feel what his heart is saying. *I missed you.*

"My bed is too hard. I haven't gotten any sleep since you left." *I missed you, too.*

Our eyes communicate what we're feeling. We look like an advertisement ourselves, his dark European good looks against the staunch conservatism of my proper high-necked blouse and pencil skirt. He follows my gaze down to where my bottom is pressed against his groin. His cock hardens and I hum in delight and push back against it.

"I could take you just like this." His head lifts and our eyes meet again in the mirror. What he sees there must please him because he smiles craftily and walks over to the door, flipping the top latch with a loud click.

I shake my head rapidly, knowing already that protesting it is pointless. He hasn't even been gone that long but already I feel like an addict in need of a fix. I could deny it all day but we both want this. Need this.

"Put your hands on the sink." He folds me over the cool surface of the counter. Already I can barely breathe, taking quick, uneven breaths as his hands trail over my back. He lifts my skirt.

"*Dio*, your scent drives me crazy." He pulls my panties down my legs, supporting me as I step out of them. Then he brings the cotton to his nose and inhales. "If I could bottle this I would make a fortune."

He tucks my panties in the interior pocket of his suit jacket and I already know I won't be getting them back. Forcing me to work the rest of the day bare-assed is the kind of thing that would amuse him. He'll no doubt find it a fitting punishment for not going with him and forcing us both through the torment of being apart.

"Spread your legs." He steps closer, bracing my legs

wider. It's so quiet I can hear the sound of his zipper going down and then the crinkle of foil as he unwraps a condom.

I start to tremble. *Oh my god*, are we really doing this here?

"We shouldn't be doing this. It's too risky."

"It's been too long," he mutters. "I can't go this long without you again."

With one thrust, we connect and I cry out at the sudden, shocking invasion. He pulls back and strokes into me again, moaning into my ear the whole time. With his back covering mine, his arms holding me down, I feel completely overpowered. Completely overwhelmed.

"Say you'll stay with me." He reaches between us, the heel of his hand tight against my clit. A hot coil of pressure builds beneath his hand, spiraling between the hard pistoning movement inside me to the gentle rocking pressure of his palm. He commands my body in a way no one else ever has.

He also holds the key to my heart as if it's a treasure box only he can unlock.

He grips my hair and the bite of pain only sharpens the pleasure as he powers into me from behind, riding me hard, pushing us both to our limits. I stare, mesmerized, at our image in the mirror. He looks carnal, with the long, curling strands of my hair wrapped around his fist, whereas I look sultry with kiss-swollen lips and flushed cheeks.

If I could take a snapshot of this image I would, just to

prove our passion is really this intense. Then he flicks his finger in a certain way and the sensation sends me hurtling over the edge.

I'm trying to be quiet but it's impossible when something feels this good. I bite his arm to stifle the sound. He groans and nips my ear.

"Sorry. I didn't mean to do that."

He chuckles softly, resting his forehead against my back. "You can bite me anytime. You make me crazy." He smooths my skirt down over my thighs.

"You make me crazy too," I whisper.

Suddenly things are awkward, standing with him in a bathroom of all places, with the smell of sex all around us. "I need my panties back."

"You'll get them back. Tonight." Andre grins and pats the pocket of his jacket. "In the meantime, their absence will remind you of me."

He holds my head in his hands so I can't avoid his eyes. "I want you to move in with me."

"Move in with you?"

"Don't say no right away. Just think about it. We'll talk more tonight." He kisses me then, a soft brush of his lips, before he backs away.

"I'll leave first. I don't want to embarrass you. Plus, I should at least show my face in this meeting since I requested it." He winks and then he's gone.

The door swings shut behind him and I hurriedly clean up before adjusting my skirt. The cool air in the room makes it even more obvious that I'm missing panties. Which was probably exactly what he intended.

He wants me to move in with him.

How did we go from one night to friends and now to sharing an address? Other people can live with someone casually but I'm not that sophisticated. Where I come from, living together is still a little taboo even if you're engaged and getting married.

I don't want to imagine what my mother would think if she found out I was shacking up with a man I haven't even been dating that long.

The work day will be over soon and he'll be expecting me at the penthouse. Which means I have between then and now to decide what to do.

A few hours later, I step off the penthouse elevator to find Andre waiting for me. I follow him inside and go through my usual evening routine, taking off my shoes and my bra, before pulling my hair down from its bun. I've gotten so comfortable being with him in the evenings that I didn't even realize how much I would miss that routine until it was disrupted.

It's amazing how fast I got used to being an everyday part of his life.

"Welcome home." Finally I can do what I wished I could earlier. I jump into his arms and he staggers slightly to keep from falling.

"I felt very welcome earlier," he murmurs.

"That can never happen again, by the way. My coworkers could have heard us. Someone could have seen you leaving the women's bathroom right before I did. That was way too risky."

He squeezes my leg. "I know. It was selfish of me to come to your workplace knowing what would happen. You have every right to want to keep things professional there. In my defense, I think I was delusional after not seeing you for so long."

"It was four days." But I'm smiling, too. Four days without him felt more like four months.

"We definitely need to talk about a few things."

"After dinner."

"Casey—"

"That's not a deflection, I promise. I'm just working through a few things in my head. We're going to talk about this."

I can feel his eyes follow me as I wiggle down and walk into the kitchen. If we're going to have a heavy relationship conversation, I'm not doing it on an empty stomach.

Completely at home, I pull open the refrigerator and whistle softly under my breath. It's crammed with food, enough to feed an army.

"I think you went a little overboard with the groceries." I gesture to the overflowing shelves.

Andre peeks over my shoulder and chuckles. "I have a part-time housekeeper who stocks the fridge for me whenever I've been out of town. I guess she figured I'd be hungry."

"I'll say. This is more food than you could eat in a month."

His phone rings and he sighs, then kisses the side of my head. "Pick out what you'd like and I'll help you after I take this call."

"You mean you'll watch me," I tease. Another thing I learned spending so much time with him is that grilled cheese is pretty much the only thing he can cook.

I roll up my sleeves. After a quick glance through the bottom drawer of the refrigerator, I line up onions, bell peppers and garlic cloves. I'm pulling out a few spices when I hear Andre's voice again.

"Jason, this can wait until tomorrow, no? Or call Philippe. He just got back in town so he can handle it. I have company. Very beautiful company. "

He's standing in the middle of the living room, his phone cradled between his shoulder and his ear while he cuffs his sleeves. I take a moment to appreciate the view. What is it about a man in a dress shirt with the sleeves rolled up?

Most unexpectedly sexy thing ever.

"Casey is here and I would very much like to get back to my guest. You understand, of course." There's a moment of long silence before his face twists into a scowl. "Yes, we're at the penthouse and no, you cannot come over."

He looks up and catches my eye. "I want her all to myself."

I look at the package of meat. It's filet mignon. Of course it is. Well, I don't know how to make anything too fancy so I can only hope it tastes good broiled with onions, the way I usually make steak.

"How about this?" I hold it up and he nods absently.

"Jason, I'm hanging up now. The woman I love is cooking for me and I'm not missing a moment of that to talk about business." He hangs up and tosses his phone on the couch.

Meanwhile I feel as if I've just been punched in the chest. "What did you just say?"

He looks at me quizzically. His brow furrows and then his hands still, his fingers stuck in the knot of fabric at his throat.

"I said I love you. That wasn't how I wanted to tell you. I had a whole thing planned. It was going to be romantic with an orchestra and some fireworks. Maybe a mime."

"That was pretty good, actually."

"Was it? Because you deserve the best, Casey. And I want to be the one who gives it to you."

I drop the meat on the counter and walk slowly back into the living room, aware the next few minutes could change both of our lives.

"You asked me to move in with you. It's a big step."

His eyes are tender as he holds out his hand. "It is. It will change your life in so many ways. Not all of them positive. People will take pictures of you and post mean things online. Just because they can. I've gotten used to living this way but that doesn't mean I don't know how much I'm asking you to give up. Maybe I'm a selfish bastard for even suggesting it. But then I never claimed to be a nice man. Just a man who loves you."

He's repeated all the negative things that I've been thinking. But when I was thinking about all the negatives, I didn't know he loved me. That changes everything.

And it's not like living here will mess with my career or my education. The penthouse is actually closer to the Mirage office and I take online classes so living here wouldn't interfere with my degree. Plenty of people will disapprove. His mother is definitely not my biggest fan. But it's really no one else's business.

"My answer is yes. This whole thing is crazy but I love you too so I'm not fighting it anymore. So yes. I'll move in with you. For as long as you want me."

He picks me up and swings me around. "I guess that means you won't be leaving ever." Reverently, he pushes my hair back from my face. "My beautiful Casey. The one who got away and then came back."

I smile then because I *feel* beautiful, here in the rapidly fading sunlight with the man I love. Mya was right. I don't want to be dumb about something that matters this much.

He's already proven he's nothing like the men I've known in the past. Being with him isn't a threat to my independence or my education. Andre has been nothing but attentive to my needs and will probably cheer the loudest when I graduate with my degree. He really is the classiest man I've ever known.

Elegance isn't just the clothes he wears. It's *him*. His nature. His clothing is just an extension of the way he naturally lives his life.

"That's what's wrong with the campaign."

I look down at him, casually sophisticated even while wearing a slightly rumpled dress shirt with his tie hanging loose around his neck. A picture of him like this would sell anything.

"What are you thinking?" He gazes at me adoringly.

"I just figured out what's missing from your advertising campaign." It's such an obvious solution that it's almost comical. "You."

He frowns. "You think I should be in the ad?"

I place my hands on his cheeks and kiss him softly. "You are the true face of Lavin Couture. It's not just a style, it's your life. No one else can represent it better than the original Lavin man who started it all."

"Have I mentioned already that I'm in love with you?" he asks.

"Maybe once. But you can show me." I squeal when he races toward the bedroom with me bouncing in his arms.

Dinner will have to wait.

21

Casey

Monday morning, I whistle as I set my lunch bag down on the reception desk. Andre helped me move most of my clothes to the penthouse over the weekend. When I told Ariana that I wasn't coming back, she didn't look surprised at all. I still feel guilty about bailing on her but she assured me renting the room really wasn't about the money.

She joked that she's apparently a good luck romance charm. Everyone who lives with her finds their soulmate and then gets married.

I laughed but it made me think.

Would Andre ask me to marry him? Things have

progressed so quickly that I'm not even sure I want him to right now. I'm still adjusting to the idea of living with him and the changes that are going to happen once he makes it known that we're a couple. He told me on Sunday that he's scheduled a meeting with his internal PR team to discuss the best way to handle it. It was supposed to be reassuring but it's honestly a little weird to think we need a PR team to tell people that I'm his girlfriend.

I plop down in my chair. Time to log in to my online class dashboard and check my grades. It's just loading on my computer screen when I hear a noise. Harold Meyer, an older man in the accounting department, is standing in front of the reception desk.

"Oh, you startled me."

"I'm surprised you came to work today." He leans over the edge of the reception desk and tries to look at my screen.

Anya warned me about him when I first started. He made a few borderline inappropriate comments but once I lied and said I had a boyfriend, he left me alone. It still annoys me that I had to do that. He's easily old enough to be my father. Not to mention that he kind of gives me the creeps.

I angle it away slightly and give him a tight-lipped smile. "Of course I came to work. Why wouldn't I?"

He smirks and throws a crumpled tabloid magazine on the desk. "You've found your golden meal ticket apparently.

Why bother coming to work anymore?" He sticks his hands in his pocket and walks away whistling.

I pick up the magazine and stare in horror at a grainy picture of me and Andre walking away from his car. My arm is through his and my face is tilted up listening to something he's saying. It's unmistakably intimate.

The headline reads *Italy's Fashion King sows his wild oats with a local Cinderella!* As I read the article, my chest gets tighter and tighter. It mentions the block where the penthouse is located and where I work. And there are pictures of us, including a blurry shot of us in the bathroom here at Mirage. Someone was in the bathroom while we were having sex.

Oh dear god.

Suddenly the doors to the agency swing open and Jason Gautier walks in, followed by James and Mya. One look at their faces and I know they've seen it.

"Is Andre here yet?" Jason doesn't even bother with a greeting. He's always been polite but apparently he's past pleasantries.

I shake my head mutely. He curses and pulls out his phone.

"I can't believe people were following us around, taking pictures of us." This is exactly what Andre was warning me about but I thought that I'd have time to get ready for it. Apparently it's been happening all along.

We weren't doing anything wrong, but having my private business splashed across a tabloid makes it seem cheap and tawdry. And the article isn't even accurate! I pick it up and read it again, my blood pressure rising with every word.

"Neither of us is cheating on anyone. Why would they say that? They can't just make up lies, can they?"

Mya squeezes my shoulder. "Unfortunately, tabloids do it all the time."

"But why would they do that? I mean I'm nobody." I'm on the verge of crying.

"That's what makes it so interesting. If you were some fame-hungry actress it wouldn't have made the front page that you were dating him." Jason turns his back and launches into a stream of French.

Andre comes in then and I run into his arms. He holds me tightly and runs a soothing hand over my hair. "It's going to be fine. I should have expected this. Prepared you for it. It was negligent of me to assume that they didn't already know about you."

"I'm just sorry you have to be embarrassed."

He waves that away with a flick of his hand. "I'm hardly embarrassed. I'm used to this, unfortunately. The good news is that the media has a short attention span. In a day or two no one will even remember this story."

Jason waves him over. I leave them talking and walk over to Mya. James is on his cell phone with his back to us. I'd assumed he would be mad but his expression had seemed sympathetic when they walked in.

"James doesn't seem too upset."

"No one blames you for this, Casey." Mya squeezes my arm. "You can't control what those idiot reporters write. It's not your fault. We're going to consider this free advertising and find a way to spin it to our advantage. That's what we do. Cole Fitzgerald, our head of PR, is on his way in. Actually that's probably who James is talking to right now."

"Thank you for being so nice about all of this. And for your advice before. I'm trying not to be so dumb, as you put it."

Mya laughs. "Good. Now it's probably best if you take the day off while we sort this out. Avoid going outside. I'm sure Andre will be able to tell you the best way to avoid the paparazzi. This will all blow over soon."

She's right. Maybe that's what he's talking about with Jason. I walk up behind them to hear them talking in low tones.

"Find out who took those pictures. I want a name." Andre sounds furious.

"The investigator is already on it. Not that it matters at this point." Jason makes an irritated sound. "We need to get to the office and figure out how to spin this thing. I haven't come this far to watch you throw it all away for a piece of ass."

I gasp. Andre turns then and sees me standing behind

them. His face twists into a mask of rage as he faces the other man again.

"Apologize. Now."

Jason shoots me a look of derision. "I'm not apologizing. She may have you under her spell, but I'm still thinking with the head on my *shoulders*. No pussy in the world is that good."

The room goes dead quiet and then Andre swings, his fist connecting with Jason's jaw with a loud crack. Jason tumbles into a side table before jumping up and charging at Andre. I scream as they fall backward into the wall, punching and kicking. Mya grabs my arm and pulls me out of the way.

An ear-splitting whistle cuts through the air.

"What the hell is going on here?" Anya stands with her hands on her hips surveying the men sprawled on the floor. Andre gets up and walks over to me.

I shake my head and back away. "Please, I can't talk right now. I just need a minute alone."

His face falls but he nods and then walks out the front doors, Jason trailing a few feet behind.

Anya picks up the pieces of a ceramic bowl that was broken in the scuffle. "The good stuff always happens when I'm late." She tosses the broken pottery in the trash can.

"Oh, you didn't miss much. Just a tabloid story with yours truly on the cover. Also the entire Lavin account is now in jeopardy because someone sold compromising pictures of us to the tabloids."

Anya gestures to the mess on the floor. "Does that have anything to do with the boxing match I just witnessed?"

I snort. "That was just the encore, where my lover's best friend told him I'm a cheap whore who's not worth all this trouble. That's all."

Anya crosses her arms. "Hmm. Sounds like prime time television. A little over-the-top for my taste."

I walk behind the reception desk and notice my college dashboard is still open. I lean closer to see my grades from my last quiz. The "D" next to the quiz number hits me like a slap in the face. I close my eyes and take a few deep breaths.

"Anya, can you find that newspaper for me?"

She leans over and grabs it from the floor. "Here it is. Although I think calling it a newspaper is an insult to newspapers everywhere. This is trash, pure and simple."

"Look at the headline. According to this, Andre is just sowing his oats before he marries some Italian socialite."

"*Italy's Fashion King sows his wild oats with a local Cinderella.*" She frowns down at the paper. "They think they're so clever. You can't believe anything you read in a tabloid."

I shrug miserably. "For all I know, he has a penthouse just like the one here in other cities. Maybe he has a woman playing house with him in every city he travels to. *I'm in way over my head here.*"

"I'm sure he can explain, Casey. The way he looks at you ... I don't think that's an act." Anya pushes the paper away. "Don't let what some stupid tabloid reporter made up bother you. They'll print anything to sell papers."

At that moment Jason comes back in, stopping short when Anya turns to glare at him. "I just need to get my briefcase. I dropped it while I was making calls." His eyes meet mine briefly before he turns away.

"Wait!"

I run from behind the desk and stand in front of him. The last time I was fooled by a man, I ignored all the signs. Maybe if I'd been a little braver and asked a few questions, I wouldn't have been so blindsided.

I hold up the paper. "Is there any truth to this?"

Jason looks at his feet. "Not exactly."

"Not exactly? I *knew* it. He's really married, isn't he?"

Jason looks up, startled. "What? I didn't say that! He wasn't married to Marcella; they were only engaged."

I grit my teeth. "Oh? Engaged, is that all? My mistake." I walk back behind the reception desk and snatch my purse from the floor. After a moment of hesitation, I pick up the tabloid and fold it under my arm.

"Wait, let me explain. They broke up ages ago, I swear."

I point at the door. "Just leave, Jason. Please? Haven't you done enough for one day?"

Anya motions toward the door. "She needs a little time to deal with all this. Mr. Lavin will be back soon and this whole misunderstanding will be cleared up."

He looks over at me. "I really am sorry." Then he's gone.

Anya pulls me into a hug. "I meant what I said to him. I'm sure this whole thing is just a misunderstanding. Just because he was engaged to that lady at some point doesn't mean anything."

"That's just it, Anya. With some men, there's always a misunderstanding. There's always an excuse. I've seen this movie before and I already know how it ends. This time though, I'm not waiting around for the closing credits."

I pull a blank sheet of paper from the printer. "Would you give him something for me?"

I write with precision, as if the care I take writing the words will soften the blow of the contents. It was foolish to think that having what I wanted would be easy. Rich, handsome princes only come to the rescue in Disney movies.

And it seems I kissed a prince and he turned into a frog. Andre was right. We really have done everything backward.

Anya slaps a hand on the edge of the paper. "I really hope that's not a *Dear John* note."

"I'll be back later. Right now, I need to get out of here before I lose it."

I glance at the mess on the floor again, Jason's words coming back to haunt me. *No pussy is that good.* He might be an asshole but he had a point.

Andre has worked to make his business a success for years. His public image is everything and a crucial part of his success, even if he doesn't want to admit it. He's been the darling of the fashion world for years without a whiff of scandal until now.

If he loses all that because of me, eventually he'll grow to resent me. It'll be like a slow poison eating away at any life we build together. I can't allow him to throw everything he's worked for away for something that could never last anyway.

And I won't throw my pride away again for a man I can't trust.

22

Andre

AFTER WALKING AROUND THE BLOCK A FEW TIMES, I think I'm calm enough not to go for Jason's throat. I need to talk to Casey. This is the worst way to be introduced to sudden fame and I have no idea how she's handling it.

But as soon as I walk back into the agency, I know she's gone. Anya's guilty expression as she hands me a note doesn't make me feel any better, either.

The simple note brings back unpleasant memories. I unfold the plain white sheet.

I can't do this anymore. I'm so sorry. I'll come by the penthouse later to get my things.

I read the words over and over and they still hold no meaning. All that comes through for me is sadness. Finality. She's ending our relationship over lies. I can't let that happen. I sit in the lobby of the agency and I have no idea how much time has passed when I hear the sound of her voice.

"I can't believe you're still here."

She's standing just inside the doorway wearing dark jeans and a blue hoodie pulled up to shield her face. Her eyes are red. Even like this, she's so beautiful she looks like sunlight.

"There you are. I had to know you were all right but I didn't want to lead the reporters to your apartment."

"I'm sorry I left that way." Casey rubs her arms. "Everything was falling apart and I needed a minute to think. We don't really know each other at all."

"I know you." Suddenly angry, I draw her against me. She fits in the cradle of my arms perfectly. "I may not know every detail yet, but I know your heart. I know *you*."

"Why didn't you tell me you were engaged to Marcella?" Casey demands.

I pause. "Who told you we were engaged? We never announced it."

Casey's eyes close and she lets out a long, slow breath. "It doesn't matter who told me. What matters is that *you* didn't."

"No, Cassandra, please listen. I broke up with Marcella long before I met you. She's someone my mother wanted to see me with. But she was never right for me. She's definitely not who I want to be with now. That's you. Only you." I squeeze her arms gently but she steps back, out of my embrace.

"Even if that's true, I just don't know if I can do this. We're so different. Can you really see me fitting in with your family, your friends, your entire lifestyle?" She shakes her head and that's when I see the sheen of tears in her eyes. "I can't live wondering how long before you get bored with me and go back to your real life."

It hits me straight in the heart to hear her say these things. "Do you think so little of me then? You really believe that I would do that? That I would lie to you?"

"I know you'd never hurt me on purpose. You're a good man, one of the best I've ever known. But I need to do what's best for me right now. And so do you." She swipes at her eyes angrily as tears flow down her cheeks. "Maybe we were right in the beginning to say things could only be one night. And our one night is finally up."

With one last sad look, she goes down the hallway and turns into Mya's office. I'm sure they're strategizing with their own PR about how to keep this from affecting their business.

And having me camped out in their lobby probably isn't helping.

I leave, fighting the urge to rage or to punch someone else. The vultures who are no doubt taking pictures of me right now would probably love that. This day is everything I didn't want for us, my worst nightmare come to life. And the fact that people around the world are looking at pictures of us during one of our most intimate moments makes me feel like I've failed her in the worst way.

This is my fault.

I know what this industry does to people. I've seen so many friends fall apart over the years or crack under the pressure. How could I let someone as sweet and full of life as Casey get chewed up by the entertainment machine? All those assholes looking at our picture don't deserve to breathe the same air she does, but even as we speak they're making memes of us and calling her names.

Worse I can't protect her because being near me is the only reason she's at risk. I am the problem.

You would think I would have learned.

When I get home, I strip out of my clothes and change into sweatpants and the coffee stained T-shirt I haven't worn since the day I met Casey. Little did I know that pint-sized, clumsy girl would change my whole perspective and make me happy for the first time in a long time. Maybe the first time ever.

Thinking of her is getting me nowhere so I pull out the convertible sleeping bag coat I've been working on in my spare time.

By the time I look up the light has faded, my throat is dry and my head hurts. When I turn around Philippe is sitting on the sofa. It looks like he's been there for quite some time.

"I was wondering how long it would take before you noticed I was here." Philippe rises from the sofa. He looks at the coat. "You've made some changes to the design. I like it."

"Casey said that the pockets should be flatter. So that things wouldn't fall out." Why does my voice sound so rusty?

"You know you never even told me about this project until after it was approved. Casey is the only one you told. Do you know why?" He doesn't wait for me to answer. "Because you trust her. Not something you do easily."

"What's the point? I've fucked up her life. She didn't sign up to be trashed in the press. She's an innocent, Philippe. She doesn't know how to do this. The things they're saying about her ... How can I ask her to live like this?"

Philippe sighs. "I'm not saying it will be easy. But what I saw in those pictures wasn't a woman looking at a meal ticket. She loves you. Isn't that worth fighting for?"

When he leaves, I wonder if he even knows the answer. Because I don't. If my choices are keeping Casey with me and subjecting her to days like today, or letting her go, then I have no idea what to do.

For the next few days, I attempt to be patient. She's hurting right now and probably trying to avoid anything that reminds her of me. But by Friday morning, I'm done. The last time we were apart this long I ravaged her in the bathroom, the reason for this whole mess.

I need to see her.

Every one of my calls has gone straight to voicemail. None of my texts have been answered. I haven't gone to her apartment because I don't want anyone to follow me there but I'm out of options.

Living under scrutiny as long as I have has taught me a thing or two about avoiding paparazzi notice. So I go to the Lavin Couture office as if I'm just reporting for a day of work. Then I have Kate drive me to her apartment while I'm ducked down in the backseat.

"Okay, so I'll wait here until you text me again. You know, just in case ... "

"Just in case she tells me to go to hell? Thanks."

Kate looks stricken. "Sorry boss."

I climb out and walk straight to the building. By the time I get to the third floor, my palms are sweating. But I'm here so there's no turning back now. I knock on the door and wait.

Ariana opens the door wearing nurse's scrubs and eating a yogurt. "It took you long enough to get here."

"Um, okay. Is Casey here?"

She rolls her eyes. "You know what, I was actually rooting for you. I kept telling her that you were going to show up, sweep her off her feet and prove that all that tabloid bullshit wasn't worth crying over. But then a day goes by and then another. I'm actually disappointed in you."

"You're not the only one. I'm disappointed in myself. Please tell her that I love her and that I'm sorry. I'm trying to fix this."

"Fix it? Everything can't be fixed. Sometimes you're just fucked. But don't worry about Casey. I'm sure she'll be fine. She'll have a few drinks, hook up with her childhood sweetheart and then the next thing I know I'll be getting a wedding invitation. That seems to be how things go with my roommates."

The next thing I know the door is coming for my face. I have to step back or risk a broken nose.

"Well, that was helpful."

Her words about Casey crying make me feel even worse. I thought I was protecting her by staying away but obviously that was the wrong move. Now she thinks I don't care enough to fight for her which couldn't be further from the truth.

But how am I supposed to fight for her when she won't answer my calls or texts? I feel like the universe needs to help me get a clue because clearly I'm missing something.

Then I think about what Ariana said again. Like most people, she revealed more than she thought in her anger. Why would she bring up Casey spending time with her childhood sweetheart? That would only be possible in one place.

249

Her hometown.

She's gone.

When I get back in the backseat of Kate's car, she twists in the seat. "Oh no. You look worse. Did you see her?"

"No."

She slaps the steering wheel. "You know what? I have held my tongue this whole time, because it's not my place. I'm just the assistant. I'm just the person who deals with you the most and probably knows you better than your own mother. Who asks for the assistant's advice? But you are screwing this whole thing up. That girl was perfect for you and she didn't take any of your bullshit. You need her in your life."

Once she runs out of air, I lean forward and tap her seat. "I know. I finally figured that out. I just figured it out too late."

Kate blows out a breath. "Well, shit."

"Yeah."

Nothing about this feels right but I had no idea things were this bad. Meeting me has cost Casey her job and her home in the city. Now she's been forced back to the very place she was desperate to escape from. I pull out my phone and think about what I'm about to do.

Then I call her one final time and leave a voicemail.

I push open the door to the penthouse and stand quietly in the entryway. After Kate dropped me off at the office, I went back to the bar where it all started, hoping I could drink until I forgot my own name. I got as far as ordering a beer when I noticed a woman reading a copy of the tabloid that started this whole mess.

It's dark and quiet as a tomb. How could I have gotten used to her presence so quickly? Already the penthouse seems lifeless and empty, like a stainless-steel prison.

The stark décor never bothered me before but suddenly I find myself missing the pair of shoes Casey always kicked off next to the front door and the sounds of her chatter as she talked to herself while cooking. Those little touches made this cold place feel like home.

I slam the door, needing to take out my aggression on something. Anything. Two quick knocks sound on the door behind me. When I open it, Jason stands on the other side watching me with a glum expression.

That'll do nicely.

Before I can swing, he grabs my arm and kicks the door closed with his foot. "I don't think you need any more tabloid coverage, do you? Unless you feel taking another cheap shot at me is worth that?"

"It wasn't a cheap shot. I didn't hit you from behind. You had the opportunity to defend yourself."

He grunts. "That's true. I was actually the one who took the cheap shot. I shouldn't have said those things."

A long moment of silence passes as we stand staring at each other.

Finally Jason breaks the standoff. "Are you going to make me get on my knees and beg? I'm trying to say I'm sorry here. Groveling isn't something I do well, you know. I'm usually not sorry at all when I'm an asshole."

Just that quickly the animosity between us is gone. Either that or I'm just too tired to hold a grudge any longer.

"I should still hit you again. Did you see the look on her face? Nothing should ever make her feel the way your words did. I want to protect her from all the ugly bits of life. She's not just another girl to me, Jason. She's the one. The *only* one."

"I know. I saw you falling deeper and deeper for this girl and we don't really know anything about her. I didn't want you to go through what I did. Loving someone who's only using you is the worst sort of betrayal. One you never really get over. Divorce doesn't cure that." Jason's face hardens before he looks away.

I walk over to the floor-to-ceiling wall of windows. The sky mirrors my mood with dark clouds that roil in a mass over the city. Inside I'm much the same, a big ball of destructive energy waiting to strike out at the closest victim.

Because of that, I try to keep my voice calm when I reply.

Jason is one of my oldest friends and there have been enough angry words between us. Especially since I understand why my friend is so deeply suspicious of women in general.

"Every woman isn't like your ex-wife. Casey doesn't want my money. She basically dumped me because she thinks she doesn't fit into my lifestyle. She also doesn't trust me now. How did this all go to hell so fast?"

Jason's eyebrows shoot up. His mouth opens and closes a few times before he speaks again. "Wait a minute. A woman actually left you because you have too *much* money?"

He stares for another moment before breaking into laughter. The longer he looks at me, the harder he laughs until I feel a smile cross my face as well.

"What are you laughing at, you idiot? She left me."

At that, my smile falls. My sweet Clumsy Girl is out there in the world somewhere alone and I'm here. Determined to stay away from her because it's the only thing she's ever asked of me.

I'd give her anything she asked for, anything she needed. Even if it kills me to stay away.

Jason claps me on the back. "She didn't really leave, you big sap. If she didn't love you, she wouldn't care about any of this. She'd just take what she could get for as long as she could get it. She's just afraid."

"So, she loves me, she just doesn't want me with her? What am I supposed to do with that?"

"What you're supposed to do is make her come to you. And I know just how to make that happen. She thinks you're keeping her as some dirty little secret, right? Like you're ashamed of her? Well, it's a good thing you have access to a billboard. Call the art department." Jason makes an impatient gesture with his hands when I don't move fast enough.

"The art department?" I pull out my cell phone and dial my marketing director automatically. "What am I supposed to tell them?"

Jason smiles and rubs his hands together. "Tell them you need a picture of the most beautiful woman you've ever seen. As big as they can make it."

A slow smile crosses my face as I realize what he's suggesting. "Make her come to me, huh? Well, it's worth a try. If this works, I'll consider us even."

23

Casey

As usual, morning comes too early and I'm caught between wanting to pretend I'm still asleep and getting up so I can get some housework done for my mom. Decisions. Decisions. I really want to help my mom out around the house while I'm here but this bed feels so good.

I convince myself that five more minutes won't hurt. Thirty seconds later I concede defeat. My mind is already awake.

When I open my eyes, I smile at the image of my favorite band when I was in high school. "Good morning, Harry. How's it hanging, Niall?"

The poster tacked on my ceiling has been there for almost ten years now. At this point it's a classic. Maybe I should have it framed.

These guys are the only reason I've been getting any sleep at all since I came back home. Being in my old room gave me a sense of safety that I definitely needed. There's no chance any reporters or paparazzi will show up in Gracewell. People here might be judgmental but when the chips are down, we don't like outsiders messing with one of our own.

Any reporters that step foot in the city limits are at risk of getting a round of buckshot in the ass. Or at least that's what Mr. Hillcrest who lives right outside the city limits always threatens when anyone bothers him.

I check the alarm clock next to the bed. It's still early. My mom won't be awake for hours. She's still working the night shift so I only see her in the afternoon. When I first arrived, she wanted to request time off so she could stay home with me but I made her promise not to. There's no reason she should burn through her vacation time when really, the decisions I need to make, I have to make alone.

After a quick shower, I walk down the hall to the kitchen. The coffee pot has already come on automatically so I pour a cup. I'm in the mood for chocolate chip pancakes so I pull out the ingredients as quietly as possible and start mixing.

It's so weird to have time to make a leisurely breakfast but I guess I should enjoy it while it lasts.

James was very kind when I asked for a leave of absence. When I first approached him I was sure that he would just suggest that I don't come back at all. But surprisingly, he was very understanding and seemed personally offended that the person who sold the picture must be a Mirage employee. He assured me they're doing everything they can to help Andre's investigator nail down the culprit but I kind of tuned out at that point.

I'm trying really hard not to think about Andre at all.

I'm in the middle of frying bacon when my mom comes in.

"That smells wonderful."

"Morning, Mom. I'm sorry if I woke you. I was trying to be quiet."

"You were. But I was already awake."

She takes out a bowl of fruit and cuts some for both of us. I plate the pancakes and then put two pieces of bacon on top of each. We sit at the small dinette in the kitchen.

"It's been so nice to have this time with you, even if I hate the reason why. When do you have to go back?"

"Tomorrow. When everything happened, my boss told me to take the rest of the week off. I thought that was pretty generous."

"It was. They're paying you even though you're not working?"

"Yeah. They've been really good to me there. And I'm

learning a lot." Neither of us mentions what else happened last week. "But I'm going to miss you. It's been nice to be home."

"Home will always be here, Casey. But hiding out won't make your problems go away."

"It was so awful, Mom. All those people online posting hateful things. I just don't know if I can live like that."

"The question is can you live without him? Because that's what's at stake here. You looked at that man like you were in love. Are you willing to let hateful people who hide behind their keyboards dictate your life?"

"It's not just about my life. What if he'd asked me to marry him?"

"Did he?" she asks with alarm. "You're so young, Casey."

"No. No marriage proposals!" I rush to assure her, not wanting her to think that I'd keep a relationship that serious a secret. "But I really like him. Eventually it might have gotten to that point and what then? If the tabloid articles are this bad when I'm just the random girl he's dating, how bad would it be if we got engaged? Would reporters start bothering my roommate? My old friends from school? *You?* I didn't know where it would end. You've already been through so much. Having me ruined all your dreams but you've made such a great life for yourself now. I don't want anything to mess that up."

She puts down her fork. "Casey, you may have changed my dreams but you didn't ruin them. Even though your father leaving me hurt, I got the best part of him. I got you. Sometimes I worry that what happened to me made you afraid to fail. But no one learns to walk without falling a few times. As long as you get back up and keep going, it'll all work out. Don't run away from a chance at happiness."

"Running away seems to be what I do best."

She pats my hand. "Maybe it's time to change that. Just think about what I said."

She moves around the kitchen cleaning up before going back to her room to shower. I do some laundry and then vacuum the living room. Since she'll be going to work soon, I slip a few hundred dollars into her wallet behind some coupons. Hopefully she won't notice until I'm gone.

But all the while I'm doing as I promised and thinking about what she said. Before that stupid tabloid article, I was happy. I was ready to take the leap and then at the first sign of trouble, I bolted. Is my mom right?

Am I afraid to fail?

Andre is everything I've ever wanted. Have I gotten so used to things going wrong that I can't even enjoy it when they're finally going right? Because even though the situation was bad, our relationship was good.

So why didn't I have more faith in us?

❧

Saying goodbye to my mom the next afternoon is really hard. But it's almost time for her to go in for her shift and I really need to get on the road. It's only four hours back to DC but I need to give myself time to return the rental car. Then hopefully I can get to the apartment and get some sleep before work tomorrow.

My reprieve is officially over.

"You call me as soon as you get back to the city. Don't forget." She squeezes me tighter. "I love you, Casey. It's all going to work out honey, you'll see."

After another round of hugs and a few tears, I manage to get out of the house. My small duffel bag goes in the backseat before I carefully back out of her driveway. I'm out of practice at this driving thing. I got the insurance on the rental car but the last thing I want is to have an accident on top of everything else.

On the way down Main Street, I stop at the coffeehouse to get something to keep me awake on the road. As I walk inside, I take in the renovated interior. Java Joes has been here since forever and I've never seen it look so good. It's owned by a man named Joe who had a daughter a grade behind me in school. She always used to work here in the summers and give the kids from school free drinks. The memory makes me smile.

There were hard things about growing up in Gracewell but there were good things, too.

"Casey? Casey Michaels?"

The brunette approaching me looks really familiar but I can't quite come up with a name. Until she smiles and then it hits me.

"Ginger Evans? Wow, I haven't seen you in ages."

We hug and she looks me over from head to toe. "I just moved back to town. You look great. Your mom said you've been working in the city. That's so exciting. Or at least it sounds that way to me since I usually spend my days covered in barf and wearing the same yoga pants that I've already been wearing for three days straight."

Her description of her life makes me crack up. "I've seen your kids on Facebook. They're adorable so I'm sure the barf days are worth it."

She grins. "Totally worth it. So how long are you in town?"

"I'm actually on my way back."

"That's too bad. I wish I could have gotten some of our old friends together for drinks or something. Everyone's missed you."

I raise an eyebrow. "The same people who gossiped about me being a home wrecker? The ones who believed Bob, *the Car Wash King*, over me?"

Ginger rolls her eyes. "Every damn body in this town

knows Bob is a pervert. No one believed him. They just gossip because there's nothing else to do."

"I bet they're having fun gossiping about me right now, too."

She winces. "I wasn't going to mention it. That article was terrible. But at least your boyfriend is hot."

That makes me laugh. "You haven't changed a bit, Ginger."

She pats my arm. "Seriously, don't let the busybodies get you down. None of us would ever do anything interesting if we listened to what other people say."

"You know what, you're right. And I think I needed to hear that today."

"Well, it was good to see you." She orders her coffee and then waves as she leaves.

I get my latte and then carry it back to my car. My eyes wander over to my bag where I've kept my phone this past week. After the first two days, I turned it off. I couldn't stomach seeing all the calls from Andre's number. My resolve was weakening and I knew I'd eventually cave and answer.

But it's time now.

As soon as I turn the phone back on and it gets a signal it lights up like a firecracker with red flags indicating all the calls, voicemails, texts and emails I need to read. I go straight to the voicemails since there's only one of those. It's from Andre.

Casey, I'm so sorry.

This is exactly the type of thing I wanted to shield you from. So even though I don't want to, I'm going to do what you asked me to in the beginning. Leave you alone.

I love you.

Tears stream down my cheeks the whole way back to DC.

24

Casey

After dropping off the rental car, I'm way too tired to deal with the metro so I take a cab back to my apartment. The lights are on so I know Ariana's home. I'm sure she'll be happy to see me doing something other than cry.

I unlock the door to find Ariana and Mya curled up on the couch watching a movie. When she sees me, Ari reaches out and pauses whatever's on the screen.

"You're back!"

I'm stunned when Ariana jumps up and walks over to hug me. Finally she says, "I'm not used to feeling all these emotions. Hug me back before it gets weird."

Laughing, I hug her before dropping my duffel bag at my feet. "I actually missed you while I was gone. Imagine that. My mom got a kick out of hearing some of my stories about you."

Mya shakes her head. "Was she worried that you're rooming with a serial killer?"

"After that tabloid story she was worried I'm selling my virtue to every businessman I meet."

Mya winces. "Oh man. That must have been a hard conversation."

"You have no idea. But things are good now. She gave me the kick in the pants I needed to get back to my life and stop running away from my problems. Which means I should probably stop being a coward and actually call Andre back."

Ariana snorts. "No way. We haven't forgiven him yet."

"Because it's all about you, right?" Mya throws one of the pillows from the couch at Ariana. "You should have gotten better at this since I needed you."

"I am good at this. I did my part. I yelled at him when he came by," Ariana says.

"He came here?" I grab Ariana's arm. "When was that? What did he say? Did he come back?"

"Whoa, first loosen your talons, woman!" Ari peels my fingers from her arm. "And it was Friday. Way too late by the way. That's what I told him. I felt kind of bad for him at the end. Hot men who are sad just get hotter somehow. It's not fair."

"No. It's not." I sink down onto the couch between them. "And he left a voicemail saying that he's going to leave me alone now. That this isn't what he wanted for me and that he loves me."

"Do you believe him?" Mya asks.

"I honestly don't know. How do I distinguish between what I want to believe and what's actually true? All that crap in the tabloid article about the women in his past was a huge wake up call. I just know I can't keep running. Eventually I'm going to have to see him again and I need to be ready to handle it."

"Oooh, it's going to be so hot when you see him again. All that sexual tension while his eyes smolder at you in Italian. Or you could just look at him on Instagram like all the rest of his thirsty fans." Ariana pulls out her phone.

Mya screeches. "You can't show her his Instagram, Ari. I don't think that's helpful when going through a breakup."

"What's the big deal? She's trying to figure out how to deal with seeing him again. If she can't handle seeing him online then it's only going to be worse seeing him in person."

I crinkle my nose. "You can be really logical sometimes. And then you do things like wear a wetsuit in the house as loungewear."

Ari winks. "One day all of the weird shit I do will make sense. In the meantime, scroll on through."

She hands me her phone. Andre's Instagram profile is already displayed. I click the last picture. It was posted this morning. The background appears to be his office. He's drawing something and completely focused on it. The caption reads, *Hard at work on Lavin Couture's new evening wear line.*

It's completely impersonal and I'm sure it was written by his social media team. But even looking at this bland picture, I feel an undeniable pull. I'm supposed to be desensitizing myself to him and instead I'm just being pulled in harder.

"Why can't I stop thinking about him? Why can't I stop wanting him?"

"You've been dickmatized," Ari says sagely like she's imparting some ancient wisdom. "Mesmerized by good dick. Don't feel alone. It's happened to me before and I thought I was immune. I mean, really? Who among us has not been dickmatized at least once in our lives?"

Mya taps her chin. "She makes a good point. Great sex can make anyone do crazy things."

"But it wasn't just the sex. It was the talking. And the way he made me feel like I could do anything."

"Sounds like love to me," Mya comments.

"It was. At least for me. But after everything that

happened, I did what I always do when I'm scared. Run away."

"What are you really scared of here?" Mya asks. "Because I don't think it's just the fact that those pictures were published. They were terrible, of course. But they were blurry and you couldn't really see much. Somehow I don't think a blurry shot of bathroom sex is really what this is about."

"He tried to prepare me for how bad public life can be but I don't think I *really* understood how famous he is. It's one thing to know that he has ten million Instagram followers. It's another thing to have those followers leaving hate comments and calling you a slut. Saying that you're not pretty enough to be with him."

"You know those bitches are just jealous, right?" Ariana interjects. "Just checking. Because they're all jealous. Hell, *I'm* jealous. You got it on with one of the hottest men on the planet so no matter who you were, they were going to say those things."

"I get that."

Mya squeezes my hand. "But that's not what this is really about. You're worried he's secretly thinking those things, too. That maybe he's just having some fun while he's in town and he's going to go back to dating some model when he's bored with you."

Taken aback by how accurate that is, I lean my head back on the couch. "I'm so stupid. He didn't do anything wrong and I made him feel like it was all his fault. Now he's done what I asked him to and given me space. How do I go back and say, '*Just kidding! I was being an insecure jealous cow*'?"

When I'm done, Ariana rolls her eyes. "Why is everyone in love so annoying? First this one—" She points at Mya. "—and now you, too. Love is a disease."

"Don't listen to Mistress Bitterness over there. Underneath her skepticism and hatred for all things emotional, she really wants you to be happy. Which is why we are going to distract you with the breakup cure." Mya hops up and heads into the kitchen.

"What is the breakup cure?" I ask.

Ariana grabs the remote again. "It's the time-honored tradition of eating ice cream and watching tons of chick flicks."

Mya comes back with several pints of ice cream, three spoons and then grabs the blanket hanging over the edge of the couch. "Things will work themselves out. I truly believe that. But tomorrow is soon enough to start being responsible and strong. Today, we eat ice cream."

I accept the spoon Ariana hands me. Going back to work tomorrow is definitely going to be strange but I plan to walk into the office with my head held high.

Then I can start figuring out how to start running to Andre instead of away.

Walking back into Mirage isn't the dramatic movie entrance I thought it would be. In my head I'd planned out how I'd walk bravely through the doors and sit proudly behind the reception desk with my head held high against any criticism.

In reality, I walk in and no one notices or cares.

It's refreshingly normal. As Mya reminded me last night, we live in the age of the twenty-four hour news cycle. No matter how big of a splash something makes, it's quickly replaced by something else.

"Welcome back." Anya rounds the edge of the front desk and leans on the counter next to me.

"Thank you. I'm glad to be back. Although I'll miss having my mom's cooking."

Anya pulls a brown paper sack from her bag on the floor and holds it out to me. "Maybe this will help then. I brought beignets from that place you like."

I squeal and rip into the bag immediately. I pop a beignet in my mouth, where the soft pastry melts on my tongue like butter. "Man, these are better than sex. Who needs men when you have melt-in-your-mouth French pastries?"

"Would you say that if you knew Mr. Lavin was asking about you the other day, I wonder?" Anya smiles craftily when I swivel around to face her. "Well, that got your attention, didn't it?"

"Andre was here? What did you say?" I narrow my eyes. Anya is quirky enough to do or say just about anything.

"He wasn't here. He called last week to finalize plans with the marketing team for the press conference today. Before I transferred his call, he asked if I'd heard from you. If you needed anything."

She leans against the file cabinet and crosses her long legs. "I think he was trying to find out when you'd be back without being totally obvious."

"I'm sure he was just making polite conversation." I tuck a stray curl behind my ear and try to look nonchalant.

"Maybe. But I saw the way he looked at you ... I even like the way he says your name. *Cassandra*," she purrs, rolling the "r" the way Andre does. She lets out a dramatic sigh and pops another pastry in her mouth.

"I figured you two would have worked it all out by now." She taps the heel of her black stiletto against the carpet. It makes a soft scratching sound every time it hits the floor. "I guess that means the sex wasn't that great, huh? Which is surprising because that bathroom picture was hot."

I choke slightly and then gulp down the piece of beignet that was stuck in my throat. "For the record, the sex was amazing. I just thought some time apart would be good for us. To make sure he's thinking with a clear head. With the head on his *shoulders*, as his friend pointed out."

"That guy was a jerk." Anya makes a face.

"Yeah, but he's saying what a lot of people are thinking. My *mom* even saw that article. She thought I was prostituting myself to pay the bills."

"But we know the truth. And personally, I'm putting my money on Mr. Lavin. I wouldn't be surprised if he calls again today."

The thought makes me smile. After my night of ice cream therapy with Mya and Ariana, I feel like I'm ready to see him. Maybe tonight after work I'll call him and we can talk. My insecurities won't disappear overnight but that's something I'll have to work on.

James passes by and waves. "Casey, welcome back. The Lavin press conference is about to start. Anya, I need you. Uh, Casey you can sit this one out if you want. Considering the circumstances."

Anya chuckles once he's gone. "Well, that was awkward. Come on. The press conference is being televised so everyone's in the boardroom watching. It's not like you have to actually see him in person. This is the first project you've assisted on so you should be there for the formal announcement. Then we can sneak out for a little retail therapy. I'm sure someone is having a sale."

Anya leads the way down the hall to the biggest conference room. Most of the other employees are already there. Milo is near the front, his attention on the large flat screen mounted on the wall.

After I made the suggestion that Andre star in his own campaign, he emailed the idea to Mya that night. She loved it but since the article came out right after that, I never got to see the final campaign.

It'll be interesting to see what the team has come up with.

The soft murmur of voices in the room quiets as the camera zooms in on Andre climbing the stairs to a small podium. The space behind him is swathed in large white curtains. He's no doubt planning to unveil the new campaign in dramatic fashion.

I move a little closer. It's hard to tell where he is until the camera pans out and the unmistakable image of the National Monument appears behind him in the distance.

He's still in town.

My heart dances a little in my chest. Even though he told us he was staying until the campaign was resolved, after all the drama of last week I wondered if he would return to Italy. I look down at my feet hoping no one else notices me mooning over him.

"Ladies and gentlemen, thank you for coming. It is with great pleasure that I make two announcements today." Andre leans on the podium, giving the impression of being completely at ease before the large crowd. It's only when the camera zooms in closer that you can see the shadows beneath his eyes.

"I am pleased to unveil the new face of Lavin Couture."

There's a dramatic flourish as the large, white sheet on the left is yanked down to reveal a stunning ten-foot photo of Andre. There's a moment of shocked silence before the audience breaks out into cheers. Andre chuckles and bows in response.

"After much debate, someone very dear to my heart pointed out an obvious truth." He pauses and stares directly into the camera. "This beloved woman told me that I was the essential ingredient that makes Lavin Couture what it is. It is an extension of my personal style and up until this point, it was my whole life. Not anymore."

The reporters in the crowd jockey to get closer to the stage, shouting questions and waving their hands in the air. He pointedly waits until they stop shouting.

"Last week I was the subject of a vicious tabloid article. It included pictures that are a shocking violation of my privacy and while I am used to being the target of such gossip, the woman I love isn't. I am done allowing the press to use scare tactics and lies to sell papers."

The crowd is quiet.

"The article contained many falsehoods but the one I want to correct is that I was cheating. I am not engaged and Miss Michaels is the only woman in my life. I love her very much but this entire thing has understandably scared her off. However, unlike most men who want to make a grand gesture, I have access to a billboard."

A second later, the other sheet is pulled away. The picture on the billboard is of a brunette with wild curls, a perfume bottle in the shape of a lotus flower perched in her outstretched hands like an offering.

"So I give you the first Lavin perfume, in honor of the woman I hope will be my future. Casey's Dream."

Everyone in the room turns around to gape at me and I cover my mouth with my hands.

Is that really how he sees me?

But I know it is. It's been there from the beginning in every touch, every word and every kiss. He has shown me that his love for me is true in every way possible. I just wasn't hearing it because I wasn't ready to believe it.

There's nothing to stop us from being together except fear. Fear of what might happen. Fear of how others will react. But what I didn't consider back then was that the fear will be countered by joy.

The joy of going to sleep with him.

The joy of waking up with him.

Every day with him will be an adventure. It'll be the two of us against the world.

Anya hugs me from behind as everyone else looks back at the screen in amazement. "I told you I was putting my money on him. When men are cheating they hide the relationship. They don't go on television and tell the world you're the love of their life. The man just named his first perfume after you. Are you really going to let him get away?"

"Not a chance."

I pull out my phone and quickly type out a text. My thumb hovers over "Send" for a moment before I press the button.

"Anya, I hate to tell you this but it looks like you're going to be covering the phones by yourself again for a while."

She heaves a sigh. "Story of my life."

25

Andre

I STAND AWKWARDLY IN THE MIDDLE OF CASEY'S LIVING room. Her message just said *Meet me at my place. I'm ready to talk.* I thought the call was a good sign until I showed up and the door was opened by Ariana.

She pointed me toward the couch and told me to wait. But I suppose she's getting ready to go to work because her demon baby is currently on the couch and I'm not sitting next to that thing.

The door behind me opens again and Casey comes in. "You're here. I didn't think you'd get here before me."

"I came straight here when I saw your message."

She looks between me and the couch. "Let's go to my room so we can have privacy."

I follow her down the hall to her room and wait while she closes the door. We stand awkwardly for a few seconds before she takes a deep breath.

"I saw the press conference. I can't believe you named your perfume after me. It's overwhelming. I really don't know what to say."

Madre di Dio.

I hope she didn't only call me here to say thank you. I don't want her gratitude. I want her to look at me the way she used to, with those shining eyes that made me feel like I could conquer the world.

"I'm so sorry for the things I said to you. The things I accused you of. You deserve so much better than that. So much better than me." She whispers the last bit so softly I almost don't hear it. It breaks my heart that she could even think it.

"There is *no one* better than you." I kiss her forehead, my lips lingering until she finally leans into the embrace.

All at once, the stress of the past week falls away and my soul is at peace again. I hold her against my heart. If words can't convey how I feel maybe the beat of my heart can bang out the message.

Or maybe I should just refuse to ever let her out of bed, then she might start to get the idea.

"Casey, you were wrong about a lot of things, but your words made me think. We do come from different worlds."

She swipes under her eyes with her sleeve. "We really do."

I walk to the window and peer outside. She follows and looks over my shoulder. All I can see is the side of another dingy building and the rusted stairs of a fire escape. "My Milan flat has a much better view. It's on the Piazza del Duomo."

She flinches. "Really? Isn't that the famous town square in Milan?"

Her lack of money and social status doesn't matter to me but it obviously bothers her so what I say in this moment is pivotal. I'll never again allow the cruel words of others to hurt her. Where I come from, a man takes pride in protecting and providing for his wife.

I close my eyes and let the word roll through me.

My wife. *Mi amore.*

I take her hand and squeeze. "Yes. It's really a beautiful building, too. With marble floors and the most exquisite architectural details. It's such a shame that I won't be keeping it."

I pull out my phone and hit the second speed dial. "*Ciao*, Philippe. I'm giving you my flat in Milan. Ask Mamma for the ... "

The phone is snatched from my hand mid-sentence.

"Are you crazy? You can't just give away a condo." She

taps hurriedly at the screen of the phone. "Sorry, Philippe," she calls out before finally disconnecting the call.

"I was going to give him the car I keep in Milan as well." I tuck my hands innocently in my pockets as she stares. "If my family is not accepting then we probably won't go there too often. Besides, maybe you will feel more comfortable with me if I am less rich, no?"

She laughs then, a full throaty sound. "I'm starting to think I'll never be comfortable with you. Perhaps that's a good thing. I'll never be bored."

"If I was a poor man, I couldn't love you any more than I do. Does any of the rest really matter?"

She rests her head against my chest. "You make it seem so easy. Nothing in my life has ever been easy. I'm afraid to believe in this."

I tip her chin up and kiss her softly. "Did it ever occur to you that I too am afraid? You might decide to love someone else and break my heart."

Casey snorts and gives me her first genuine smile. "Not happening. I can't imagine loving anyone else."

I lean down until our noses touch. "It's going to be a transition but I believe in us. And there are things we can do to make the transition easier."

"What's that?" She reaches up and threads her fingers through my hair. She's touching me all over. I think she's missed this almost as much as I have.

"Well, you could move back into the penthouse like we'd originally planned. My personal security will be able to protect both of us better if we're in the same place."

She nods. "Moving back in is a definite yes. Because all my clothes are there and I'm not packing all that stuff back up. What else?"

"I can turn off the comments on my Instagram posts. It won't stop all the trolls but at least we won't have to see it."

"You don't have to do that. Let them rage. As Ariana pointed out, they're just jealous. And it's not like I can blame them. I would be jealous, too."

I bury my face in her hair. "There's one more thing that would really shut up the haters. Something that would show the world that I love you and I'll never stop."

Her breath catches as she finally realizes what I'm leading up to.

"Marry me, Cassandra."

She puts a hand on my cheek. "You don't have to marry me to keep people from talking. I'm not running away anymore. Let them talk. As long as I have you, I'm happy."

"You think that's why I'm asking you?"

"You're worried about me. You're very sweet."

"I'm not sweet. I'm a man with an obsession. You've gotten away from me twice before. And I never want to lose you again."

She looks thoughtful. "I'll make you a deal. Let's take

some time and let things settle. Then I want you to ask me again."

"Deal. That gives me time to plan a more romantic proposal. If I want to lock this thing down, I guess I'm going to need that orchestra and the fireworks. And a diamond big enough to blind anyone who gets near you."

She snuggles closer. "You know I don't care about that. Although ... "

"What?" I lean back to find her watching me closely.

"I just have to admit that you being wealthy isn't entirely a bad thing. You should have never told me about your place in Milan, you know. I've always wanted to go there. You'll never get rid of me now."

"Good. I don't want to." I kiss the tip of her nose.

"Then can we go to Milan? And Tuscany, because it looks so pretty in the movies. Oh, and I definitely have to see Rome, too."

Holding her close, I kiss her lips and then her neck. "Anything you want is yours, my love. All you have to do is ask."

THE ANSWER

Andre

I'M STILL THAT GUY.

No, really. I am. Being with Cassandra hasn't changed me, not in the sense that people usually expect. I'm still living a charmed life. Trips around the world, fast cars and yes, even faster women.

Except now those women all know that my heart belongs to the woman by my side.

Casey accompanies me on most of my business trips now. She made the decision to take some time off while she finishes her degree. I know it made her uncomfortable to put so much trust in us, but being with me isn't the kind of thing you can do halfway. She's proven to me that she's in it all the way. We're a team.

And I have no problem admitting that she's the best part of the team.

She has elevated me. Refined me. Made me more myself than I've ever been. If you had asked me a year ago, I would have said I didn't care what anyone thought of me.

But I did.

There's an expectation that you have to obtain certain things to have a good life. But money, status and power aren't the only things that matter and aren't even the things that make us happy.

For me, it's her.

Because thanks to her, I no longer feel the need to seek validation. Interesting, isn't it? That the side effect of being so completely and perfectly loved would be confidence.

Not that I need any more of that, right?

Casey tells me I'm still arrogant. But I still can't figure out why that's a bad thing. Clearly I'm pretty damn amazing to convince the most beautiful girl in the world that I'm worthy of her. There are days I still wake up and wonder when she'll finally discover that she can do better. Then she kisses me and nothing else matters.

That's the secret I was looking for all along. I kept searching for the meaning of life, trying to understand what the point of it all was. But the answer is the simplest thing in the world.

The point isn't to have the highest net worth. Or to be the most successful. Or to have the most stuff. No matter how many cars I buy or pieces of property I own, none of it matters.

That's what my father was trying to tell me all those years ago. Finding the right person, the right puzzle piece, doesn't change you. It just completes the picture. I don't have to be perfect. I just need to be perfect *for her*. And the reward for figuring it out is getting to spend the rest of your life with someone who loves you exactly as you are.

That's why I'm here.

Haven't you figured it out yet? That's why we're *all* here.

Now you know.

EPILOGUE

Casey

GETTING READY FOR TONIGHT SHOULDN'T BE THIS BIG OF a deal.

Over the past year I've gone with Andre to many events, most of them black-tie and I've become very familiar with wearing evening gowns.

It helps tremendously that each gown is breathtaking and tailored perfectly to my shape. But still, it's been an adjustment to go from my jeans and sandals to haute couture and stilettos. An adjustment I think I've navigated pretty well.

However, tonight is different. It's the 23rd annual International Fashion World Gala. Out of all the events we've attended together, this will be the first red carpet. After much discussion, Andre agreed to enter therapy to better deal with the fan attack that still haunts him.

But even with all the progress he's made, this will be the first time he has walked a red carpet since.

"We don't have to go. I'm more than happy to stay home and avoid wearing these insanely high heels."

I take a deep breath and spritz myself with some Casey's Dream. I love the scent he chose for my fragrance. It's light and summery with just a hint of vanilla.

Andre doesn't respond. I'm in the bathroom while he's outside on the bed waiting for me to finish getting ready. Of course, he took only ten minutes to dress and looks like a billion dollars.

"It would also mean I don't have to put more makeup on this stupid pimple that showed up on my forehead this morning." I wait to see if he's going to continue to ignore me.

Finally he responds. "We're getting ready to launch the next fragrance and marketing thinks this will be good PR."

"All those PR people can go to hell." Then I think about it. "Okay, not Cole. He's so nice. But all the other ones. We don't have to do anything we don't want to do."

"Cole? You mean *Mr. Fitzgerald*? Why do you call him Cole? You don't even know him."

"I know him. He's a very nice man."

He still hates it when I call other men by their first names.

Although I'm not sure why since he loves it when I call him Mr. Lavin. To be fair he's usually got me in a very compromising position when I'm calling him that. I think he'd love anything I called him.

He even gets jealous sometimes about the sexy books I read. He says he doesn't want me to have book boyfriends because he's my boyfriend. Don't tell but I secretly kind of love it. It really is cute.

Speaking of which, I definitely don't want him to see the book I brought along on this trip. It's this hot bodyguard romance Ariana recommended which would be fine if our security company didn't employ some of the hottest bodyguards in existence.

Blake Security came highly recommended. But I don't think Andre realized when he hired them that all their guards look like superheroes.

The man who escorted us to the hotel earlier was named Oskar and looks like Chris Hemsworth's brawnier cousin.

Ariana would be in heaven.

I swipe on a few more strokes of mascara, amused when Andre comes into the bathroom, still muttering under his breath about Cole. When his arm snakes around my waist, I lean back into his embrace.

It's still hard to believe a man with so many *Hottest Man Alive* magazine covers can get so jealous. But it's true and Andre may be one of the hottest men alive but he's also *my* man. He wants me all to himself and I feel exactly the same way about him.

He kisses the side of my head. "We have to attend but I really wish we didn't. I don't want to share you with the world tonight. Especially when you're wearing that dress. I'll have to fight off men left and right."

The dress is silver and drapes low in the back. Every time I take a step, the dramatic side slit flashes my entire left leg. It's breathtaking and makes me feel like a goddess.

"Mmm, it is gorgeous. But it's your fault it's so revealing."

His head lowers and his tongue traces a warm path up toward my ear. "Do you know what it does to me to see you wearing something I designed just for you?"

I shudder as his fingers start sliding south. When I move my hips, his hard erection digs into my back. "I can *feel* what it does to you."

His fingers find the zipper on the side of the dress.

The sensation of his fingers on my skin is magic but if I let this continue, then I'll end up with smeared makeup and love bites all over my neck. And since I'm not sure yet whether Andre really wants to stay home, I need to slow this train down. Because my main interest is in making sure he's happy.

"That zipper isn't coming down until I know whether we're staying in."

His smile tickles my cheek. "We're going out."

I don't understand why he's been so insistent that we

attend *this* event. I'd rather wait until he's truly ready but I think he's afraid of letting his protégé down. Timothy Armand is receiving the Best New Designer award and I know Andre is really proud of him.

"You're sure? Because Tim will understand if we don't come to see him accept his award. He's been so grateful for all your help and mentorship this year. Let's just invite him over for dinner next week. I'll make the chicken and dumplings that he loved last time."

Andre chuckles. "I promise, I'm fine. Just don't let go of my hand."

Sometimes I think this man has no clue just what he means to me. He supports my goals whether it's finishing my degree or reapplying for a job at Mirage as a junior associate. Another man might not understand why I want to work when he has the means to support me but Andre just gets it.

He just gets *me*.

I straighten his tie, even though it's already perfect. Any excuse to touch him will do. I pull him down for a kiss.

"You don't have to worry about that. I won't let go. Ever."

I won't be letting go until it's time to go to my grave.

EPILOGUE

Andre

Hundreds of camera flashes spark as we make our way down the red carpet. Casey's fingers have to be hurting since I've been squeezing her hand this whole time but the smile on her face never falls and most importantly, she doesn't let go.

"Mr. Lavin! Look this way!"

The panic starts to rise, everything about this eerily reminiscent of the last time I was on a red carpet. Everywhere I turn there are people shouting and the edges of my vision start to recede. Going out tonight was clearly a mistake.

Then Casey squeezes my arm. I look down at her and the chaos falls away and all I see is her. She puts a hand on my cheek and stands on tiptoe for a kiss.

"How did you know I needed that?"

She glances over at me coyly. "Who says I did? I just wanted to kiss my gorgeous boyfriend. If we have to pose for pictures, we might as well give them some that are worth it."

I laugh at her cheeky reply. She has uncanny radar for when I need her support and offers it unfailingly. As always, she's looking out for me.

Now I want to look out for her.

Up ahead I see Jason waiting for me. Over his shoulder I catch a glimpse of Ariana, Mya and Olivia Michaels, Casey's mother. The past week has been a blur due to all the preparations for tonight. But I want Casey to have one night that's absolutely perfect.

When we reach the middle of the red carpet, I raise my hand. At my signal, twenty people stand up from where they've been hidden amongst the photographers and start to play Pachelbel's Canon. The photographers shout at first but as the word spreads about what's happening, they settle down, waiting for what's about to unfold.

"Andre, look! It's a flash mob!" Casey squeals in delight and points at the makeshift orchestra performing beside us.

Then the first fireworks explode overhead.

She looks up in wonder. "Fireworks? I didn't know they planned fireworks for tonight."

When she turns around, I'm down on one knee holding a ring.

For the past few months, I've thought long and hard about when I wanted to propose to Casey again. Her words that day in her apartment were meaningful and revealed a lot about what she truly fears. I know that she loves me and will stay with me no matter what. But that's not what this proposal is about. At least not for me. I want her to know that I'm choosing her.

And that above all else, I desperately want her to choose me back.

"Cassandra Michaels. You are the most enchanting, exasperating, clumsy, elegant, delightful mass of contradictions I have ever met. I've had a hard year but your strength and your kindness are what has sustained me. You give me so much. And now I'm asking you for your hand in marriage. Casey, will you do me the honor of being my wife?"

"Of course, I'll marry you. I love you—"

Her answer is interrupted when a man in a black and white costume steps out of the crowd and starts performing. I shake my head as I get to my feet.

Casey giggles. "I see you didn't forget the mime."

"He was supposed to come out before the orchestra. Why

are things always backward with you?" I slide the ring on her finger before anything else can disrupt my plans.

Her eyes shine as she squeezes my hands. "Because we like to get to the good stuff first. I can't believe you did this!"

I love how surprised she is by everything. She makes even the most routine things fun. I look forward to experiencing the world through her eyes.

She's about to say more when she notices her mom in the crowd of people watching. "Oh my god, you brought my mom!"

"Of course I did. I need all the points I can get. I'm already shooting for the stars asking for your hand. You're way too good for me."

She looks around at the crowd of people watching and taking pictures. "Are you sure about this? We haven't been together that long."

There was a time when the question would have bothered me. I used to think her bouts of uncertainty were because she didn't trust me or didn't feel as deeply as I do. But now I understand that just as I have issues to work through, so does Casey. As usual my father's wisdom showed me the way. We're puzzle pieces which means we have to work together.

She will be my strength when I need it and I will be her confidence.

"I've never been more sure of anything. Most people wait their whole lives to fall in love. I only needed one night."

Her smile is so bright it could power a city. "You're never going to let me live that down, huh?"

"No. I'm still not over it. It may have only been one night but I wished it could last forever. So I'm asking you to give me all of your nights. All of your days. All of your love."

I draw her into my arms, thrilled when she pulls me down for a kiss. The photographers go wild, hooting and catcalling like teenagers. When we finally break for air, Casey blows them a saucy kiss before promptly tripping over the hem of her dress.

She's still my sweet clumsy girl.

What more could I ask for?

I hope you enjoyed reading ASK ME as much as I enjoyed writing it. Did you miss Milo & Mya's book? If so, keep reading for an excerpt of BEG ME!

And I promise no plastic cows were harmed during the creation of the book. OKAY, there was that one time. But other than that, none.

That doesn't make sense now but soon you'll understand.

Author's Note

Want a free book? (and really, who doesn't?)

Become one of Minx's Minions! I reward my evil followers well :) Click HERE

Did you miss Milo & Mya's story?

I won't just win,
I'll make her *beg*...

BEG *me*

NYT & USA TODAY BESTSELLING AUTHOR
AND 2019 RITA* AWARD WINNER

M*inx* MALONE

MYA

I want this job. And no one, especially not the office playboy is going to stand in my way. He's cocky and irritating and entirely too good-looking.
So WHY the hell did I just tell him my most shameful secret?

MILO

I want her. Not sure what I did in my past life, but it must have been bad. Because the only woman I want is my co-worker. My competition.

When I find out she's never taken a trip to O-town, we make a little wager. Not only will I win the client, but I'll prove to her that multiple's are NOT a myth.

BEG ME is a completely inappropriate romantic comedy. Side effects may include clutching your pearls and laughing until you almost choke.

Download BEG ME now

Excerpt of *BEG ME*
© March 2018 M. Malone

MYA

Considering how many things have gone wrong tonight, you'd think it couldn't get much worse, but apparently we haven't reached our quota on weirdness for the night. Standing in a hotel room alone with Milo while he talks about screaming during sex takes it to a whole different level.

Especially since the way he's watching me makes it clear he's not going to just let this go.

"Have you?" he presses again, his eyes locked on mine.

This is *not* happening. I'm not talking about orgasms while he stares at me like that. Just not doing it.

"I'm hardly a virgin, Milo."

His face twists into a grimace. "Jesus, don't say that."

"What? I just said–"

"What you said was a bullshit attempt to deflect and not answer. Which tells me everything I need to know." He runs his hands through his hair, looking pissed off, which makes no sense to me.

"How did we go from discussing your bad behavior at dinner to talking about my love life?" *My non-existent love life*, I think ruefully.

A guy like Milo probably goes through women like underwear. What would he say if he knew it's been six months since I've been laid?

Or kissed. Or hugged. Or touched.

Great, now he's got me thinking about how pathetic I am.

"I'm just trying to understand what the fuck is happening in the world that a woman like you is having bad sex. Any man lucky enough to see you naked should be putting in the work to take you to O-town every time."

Something in my expression must tip him off because suddenly he stops pacing and stares at me. "Mya, you've *had* an orgasm before, haven't you?"

Now we've crossed the line from inappropriate to just straight-up embarrassing.

"Of course, I have. Not that it's any of your business."

He still looks disturbed, but at least he's no longer looking at me like some kind of space alien, which is why I have no idea what possesses me to say what I do next.

"Just not while anyone else is there," I mumble softly.

"Fuck me!" he explodes before whirling around to blink at me in disbelief. His mouth opens and closes several times before he makes a strangled growling sound that has me going instantly wet. "Fucking hell."

"Fucking isn't the problem," I snap, mortification at what I've admitted starting to sink in.

Of all the people I could have confided in, why would I tell Milo? For years it's been my secret shame and the real reason my ex didn't want to "settle" with me. I've read every Cosmo article, tried yoga and hypnosis and even those weird-ass positions in the illustrated Kama Sutra I ordered online. William was offended when I suggested using a vibrator in bed, and he didn't even seem to like when I touched myself.

Maybe that was the problem. It all felt like work instead of fun. And right now, it just feels like one more way I don't measure up. Especially with the way Milo is looking at me.

"You know what? I'm done talking about this. It's been a long night, and we're probably both going to be out of a job tomorrow once James sobers up and comes to his senses. So for now, I'm going to my room to get comfortable."

He springs forward and grabs my arm. "Wait, Mya. I'm serious about not leaving yet. I'm pretty sure Christiane is staying on this floor. And she seems predisposed to hate us anyway."

Fed up with being told what to do, I reach behind me and unzip my dress. "I need to get out of this bra before it cuts off my circulation." I raise my eyebrows, waiting to see what he'll do.

But he shocks the hell out of me when he calls my bluff. Milo grabs one of the discarded dress shirts from the bed and hands it to me. "Change into this. You can order room service and relax just as easily here as you can in your room."

Clearly, like most men, Milo has no idea what relaxation means for a woman. But I'm just embarrassed and exhausted enough not to care anymore. So I take the shirt and escape into the safe haven of the bathroom. Once the door is closed and locked behind me, I meet my own eyes in the mirror. That was the most ridiculous conversation, but strangely cathartic, too. Maybe I just needed to tell someone, and Milo happened to be the unlucky bystander when it all came bursting forth.

Not that he should have acted like it was such a bother to him. I'm the one who's been sexually frustrated for years, after all. If anyone has cause to be annoyed by the situation, it's *me*.

The bathrooms in this hotel come stocked with all manner of toiletries, so I use the mini facial bar to wash my makeup off. There's a small hook on the back of the door, so I use that to hang my dress by the straps and put on the shirt Milo gave me. It's a good thing he's so tall or there would be no way this thing would fit over my chest, but it's just big enough. Although I have to unbutton quite a bit at the top so I don't feel like my boobs are being strangled.

After pulling the pins out of my bun, I finger comb my hair down around my face. It's super thick, so it's easier to keep it braided or in a bun, but when I'm relaxing, I just let it go wild. Milo will just have to deal. He's the one who wouldn't let me leave, so if he doesn't like it, he can bite me.

The man looked like he wanted to bite you anyway.

With that thought, I yank open the bathroom door and march back out into the room. Milo looks up from the mini bar where he's selected a small bottle. His mouth falls open slightly before he clears his throat and looks away, guiltily.

"Want a drink?"

"Uh, sure."

"We have scotch, some dubious-looking wine, and vodka."

I shrug. "Alcohol. Anything that can make me forget the past three hours."

He's about to respond when my phone rings. To my

surprise, Milo picks it up as if he has every right to know who's calling me. He tilts the screen so I can see the face. A picture of me and William taken during our last New Year's Eve flashes on the screen. I take the phone and hit the button to silence the call.

"I never got around to changing the picture on his profile," I blurt. Then I'm instantly mad at myself for explaining. I don't have to justify why I have a picture of my ex on my phone.

"He's called twice already. Some men really don't know the meaning of no, do they?"

I climb back on the bed, satisfied when Milo's eyes follow the movement of my legs. He hasn't invited me to take over his bed, but oh well. This is what you get when you stand between a girl and her chill time. I settle back against the pillows and snuggle into the cozy sheets.

"William wasn't too good at listening in general," I admit.

"Enough about him. What did you think of the rest of the Lavin team? Obviously, Christiane hates us. But otherwise?"

To my surprise, we spend the next hour talking about everything related to Lavin Fashions. It's not a surprise to me that Milo has researched their prior campaigns, but he also looked up human interest stories about the brand and found out what their charitable initiatives are. That's one that I hadn't thought of yet. Then I tell him about the collaborations

Mr. Lavin did before he started the brand. That was something Milo hadn't thought of.

And in the midst of it all, I can't help thinking that we make a pretty damn good team.

"Can I ask you something?" Milo asks when there's a lull in the conversation. We've been sitting quietly for a few minutes, but it's a good kind of silence. The comfortable kind where you don't feel any pressure to perform and you can just *be*.

"Sure. I mean you've already asked the embarrassing stuff, like how I like my orgasms. How much further down the rabbit hole can we go?"

His smile awakens something in me that I didn't know was dormant, and I press my thighs together to stop the ache. But as usual, Milo is tuned in to everything I'm feeling. His eyes drop to the juncture between my thighs, and his blue eyes darken. When he speaks, his voice is one shade above a growl.

"Why did you stay with a guy who didn't satisfy you? One who made you feel that you had to wear long skirts and hide yourself? I'm trying to understand, but I just don't get it. You're so strong. I can't imagine you taking shit from anybody."

This is the kind of conversation we probably shouldn't be having when I'm dressed in only his shirt and snuggled next to him on a bed. Maybe it's the mini-bar wine stealing away the last fucks I had to give, but I just don't care anymore.

"Even strong women get lonely," I say finally. "Will isn't a bad guy, just an oblivious one. And he wanted something I couldn't give him. Do you know what he said to me at the end?"

He turns over so he's now facing me directly. "What?"

"He said that settling down with me felt too much like settling. Like I was the consolation prize he'd accepted when he couldn't find anything better."

If you'd asked me before that moment, I'd have told you I was over it and that Will's words didn't have any power over me. But saying it to Milo in that moment was different, like I could actually admit how much it had hurt.

"And now he's trying to get you back. You know why?"

I shake my head through the tears that have suddenly sprung to my eyes.

He tips up my chin. "Because he's finally wised up and discovered how lucky he was to even have a chance with you. A chance that he won't get again. You are one of a kind, Mya Taylor. And you are no one's fucking consolation prize."

My phone rings again, and the picture of Will and me flashes on the screen. Milo looks down at the phone and then up at me. "May I?"

I have no idea what he means, so I shrug. He grabs the phone and swipes right to answer.

"Yes. No, you have the right number, this is Mya's phone. This is her fiancé."

My mouth falls open.

"That's right, her *fiancé*. A guy who is smart enough to know exactly how special she is and how lucky I am to be with her. A chance you won't have again, so please fuck all the way off and stop calling." He pulls the phone away, but then before he disconnects, he puts it back to his ear. "And by the way, pal, her kneecaps are *fantastic*."

Then he drops the phone back on the bed and his mouth crashes down on mine.

Download BEG ME now at minxmalone.com/begme

One More Day : "Good girl" Ridley has always attracted bad guys. Now she's on the run and has nowhere to hide. So when Jackson Alexander mistakes her for her twin, she decides to do something she knows is wrong. *She lies.*

The Things I Do for You : Nicholas Alexander finally has something the woman of his dreams needs. He'll give Raina a baby if she gives him what he wants. *Her.*

He's the Man : Matt Simmons is over Army doctors poking him until he sees his old babysitter, now a physical therapist, is h-o-t. Suddenly he's seeing the benefits of therapy.

All I Want: The only thing Kaylee wants is for Elliott Alexander to stop treating her like she's invisible. But a car accident forces her to reach out to the only man she trusts to save her.

All I Need is You : When the man she loves leaves town after their steamy kiss, Kaylee Wilhelm is done. But when she's targeted by a stalker, Eli is the only one who can protect her.

Say You Will : Mara Simmons has always known Trent Townsend is *The One*. But when she suspects his frequent business trips have *nothing* to do with business, she sets in motion a chain of events bigger than she can imagine and discovers that the man she loves just might be a stranger.

Just One Thing : Scientist Bennett Alexander is a bona fide genius but he still can't figure out how to "get the girl". So he hires a dating tutor. What could go wrong? Other than falling for his teacher, of course.

Bad King: My parents just put a gold diggers target on my back. But if all they want is a wedding, I can do that. I'll find the fiancee of their nightmares. *Who Wants to Marry a Billionaire? Must be completely inappropriate.*

Bad Blood : I'd do anything for my best friend's little sister. Until she asks for the one thing I can't give. One night. No rules. ***2019 RITA® Award Winner!***

Blue-Collar Billionaires

Billions from the deadbeat dad they never knew sounds pretty sweet. Until they find out what he really wants.

Tank / Finn / Gabe / Zack / Luke

- ROMANTIC SUSPENSE -

(Co-authored with Nana Malone)

- The Shameless Trilogy
- The Force Duet
- The Deep Duet
- The Sin Duet
- The Brazen Duet

- PARANORMAL ROMANCE -

Nathan's Heart

The Brotherhood of Bandits

M. Malone is a 2019 RITA® Award winner and a NYT & USA Today Bestselling author of completely inappropriate romantic comedy. She spends most days wearing Wonder Woman leggings and T-shirts that she's embarrassed for anyone to see while she plays with her imaginary friends.

She lives with her husband and their two sons in the picturesque mountains of Northern Virginia even though she is afraid of insects, birds, butterflies and other humans.

She also holds a Master's degree in Business from a prestigious college that would no doubt be scandalized at how she's using her expensive education.

facebook.com/minxmalone

twitter.com/minxmalone

instagram.com/minxmalone

bookbub.com/authors/m-malone

Printed in Great Britain
by Amazon